A LIGHT IN THE DARK

W. M. BECK, JR.

A MARLEBONNE TALE

A LIGHT IN THE DARK

TATE PUBLISHING
AND ENTERPRISES, LLC

Published by Tate Publishing & Enterprises, LLC
127 E. Trade Center Terrace | Mustang, Oklahoma 73064 USA
1.888.361.9473 | www.tatepublishing.com

Tate Publishing is committed to excellence in the publishing industry. The company reflects the philosophy established by the founders, based on Psalm 68:11,
"The Lord gave the word and great was the company of those who published it."

Book design copyright © 2013 by Tate Publishing, LLC. All rights reserved.
Cover design by Rodrigo Adolfo
Interior design by Caypeeline Casas

Published in the United States of America

ISBN: 978-1-62902-956-6
1. Fiction / Fantasy / General
2. Fiction / Action & Adventure
14.01.10

DEDICATION

For my wife, who believed in me without cause
and supported me without reason, save love.

ACKNOWLEDGMENTS

I would like to thank everyone who has contributed along the way to this book. Of special note are the folks at Dark Mists (www.darkmists.net) and Winter's Oasis (www.wintersoasis.com) who have contributed to my wild imaginings for many fun-filled years; my friend Bill who is a cohabitant of those fantastic realms; Jenny Fengler, whose proofreading and editorial critique were invaluable; and my children Morgan, Maddie, Billy, Johnny and Charlotte who daily remind me to be in awe of God.

June 11, 727 AE

My dearest Lola,

I have discovered something that may allow me to return to you. It seems like an eternity since we said our good-byes, and were it not for our great love, I would not have been able to endure it. But now, I may have found a way to come home.

A routine patrol turned up what I believe to be a Svargan ruin, some type of underground complex. We've begun to explore it and have found something truly astounding. If I can find a way to turn it all on, it could very well win this war for us. Wouldn't that be wonderful? I haven't contacted my superiors about it yet, for if I show it to them now they will just call in the scientists and I won't get any of the credit, but if I am able to deliver it to them already working—that should earn me a place of prestige. Then I will be able to return to Chevaire a hero and will have secured a future for us.

With any luck, my next letter will be to announce my success, and we can talk once again of a date to be married. I will do whatever it takes to return to you, my love.

Yours eternally,
Girard

PROLOGUE

The city of Dunham had a vibrant night life. There was a myriad of taverns, pubs, inns, and all other manner of places where someone could get a drink. The Moon Dance was no exception. Song filled the air as bottles and glasses were passed around among the patrons. There were Dogs, Foxes, Salamanders, Rats, Cats, Horses, Lizards, and every other Species imaginable.

The railway had turned the city into a bustling center of commerce, the largest on the eastern edge of Marlebonne. Until its construction, Dunham had been just a fishing town on the Sea of Veritas. Now, it was a gateway for the sea's bounty. The rich forests that surrounded it were quickly being pushed back and replaced with factories. A large coal deposit had been found to the east, not quite into the Wastes. Everything was going Dunham's way.

Brunois felt everything was going his way too. The influx of money to the city also brought an influx of Animals who were loose with it. As such, he was raking it in.

He sat at a round table toward the back of the room with two Dogs and a Rabbit playing cards. The Dogs were dressed like one would expect: simple cloth trousers and shirts without waistcoats. Their jackets were draped over the back of their chairs, dust permeating them through and through. The Rabbit was dressed more in the fashion of a gentleman, with a matching charcoal gray suit of clothes, which included a red bowtie and stovepipe hat.

"Raise ya. One hundred," Brunois croaked out, throwing the money into the pot.

The Dogs glanced at each other over their cards. The Rabbit wiggled his nose.

Brunois just waited. *This is too easy.*

The Rabbit folded with a laugh. He certainly was being a good sport about all this, considering he already lost close to three hundred lucra. "Don't think I shall fall into that one, sir."

One of the Dogs, who had a black patch of fur over his left eye, snorted loudly.

"Call, Frog," he barked gruffly, throwing his money into the pot. He gave a stern look to the other Dog who, grudgingly, also threw his money into the center of the table.

"Call too."

Brunois grinned and laid his cards down. "Full house, mates. What'chya got?"

Both Dogs threw their cards down on the table and growled. Brunois ribbited with laughter and collected his money.

"Well, gents, I think that be it fer me t'night. Been a pleasure to be playin' with ya, maybe we have us 'nother game tomorrow, eh?"

The Rabbit nodded. "Indeed, well played, sir. Have a good evening."

The Dogs only growled.

Brunois walked up to the bar, hopped up on a stool, and ordered a drink. He wanted to see what the Dogs were going to do before he left. They seemed like the sort that would just shoot him and take their money back. The city constabulary would not mourn Brunois's death.

His drink arrived and he began to sip it. The bartender was a pretty orange Salamander with big eyes. He gave her a big tip and smiled. She smiled back in the practiced way of those who make their living off tips.

Behind the bar was a long mirror with bottles lined up in front of it. Brunois tracked the Dogs' movements in its surface. They pointed at him a few times then put their jackets on and walked out the front door.

Predictable.

Brunois finished his drink, hopped back down from the stool, and headed for the back of the building. *Best to just slip out into the night and be gone.* He unbuttoned his holsters, just in case he did end up having to draw down on one of them. Or both of them.

The alley was deserted, but it did have echoes of the merriment that was being had nearby. After surveying the scene a moment and allowing his eyes to adjust to the lower light, Brunois slipped out the door and began to walk toward the other side of the block. The moon was full and the night air was crisp. The weight and feel of the money in his jacket was reassuring. He was so happy with his winnings, he almost didn't hear the steps turn the corner where the alley let out onto the main street.

He dove to the side behind some crates just in time. Bullets ricocheted off the ground where he had stood. His guns found their way into his hands. Another volley. *How foolish of them.* The pair of Dogs began to close the distance. Brunois held his breath to better make out their footsteps. When one was close enough, he hopped across the alley to another group of barrels, firing into the chest of the closer assailant as he did. The Dog went down. First to his knees then facedown into the mud. The other one waited a moment then ran. *So much for loyalty.*

Knowing it wouldn't be long before a constable came, Brunois made a quick search of the Dog's body and pack. There was something heavy in it. Brunois pulled it out; it was large and wrapped in a red handkerchief. He unwrapped it and balked a little at what he saw, but knowing this was not the time and place to study it, rewrapped it and made for the other end of the alley.

"Hey, you! Stop there!"

Spotted. And so many of the constables knew him. He would have to run fast. Brunois sprinted out the back of the alley, sticking to the shadows as much as possible. The route he ran was a familiar one. The alleys and side streets of this quarter were well known to him. The moon shone down brightly, casting reflections into puddles that shattered when his feet splashed into them. Once he was certain he had lost the constables, he circled around on his own tracks several times, just to be sure.

Having eluded all his pursuers, he proceeded to some place he might find a safe haven. *How did I manage to run afoul of both the law and a pair of Dogs in the same evening?* He shook his head and rid himself of such thoughts. They would do him no good.

His destination was a small shop made of the same wood as the buildings that surrounded it, a dark brown and weathered variety. The front windows showed no light, so he looped around to the back. There, he found a window with a slight flicker of illumination in it. No one was around, the only sound was the ambient howl of the city, which never left, only waxed or waned depending on where one stood at a given moment.

Brunois rapped sharply on the door for several seconds and then waited. A small slot opened, and beady eyes stared out of it. Brunois returned the stare. He thought he heard a faint chuckle from behind the door.

The door opened to reveal a Rat dressed in simple brown trousers and a white shirt holding a brass lantern in his hand. He looked Brunois over.

"What do you want?"

"I need to be layin' low fer a while, Gassik. Got me some interested parties followin' m'scent. I be givin' them the slip, but they may find me after all."

"Why should I help?"

Brunois held out the object he had taken off the fallen Dog and pulled the red handkerchief back to show the glint of silver underneath.

The Rat nodded, looked up and down the alleyway, and motioned for Brunois to come inside. Once he was there, he relaxed a bit and placed his cargo on a table.

The handkerchief fell away, exposing a silver and gold object that looked like a large egg.

Gassik's eyes widened at the sight of it. Brunois was equally transfixed. On its surface there appeared to be several interlocking leaves, each etched with a symbol of some type of bug.

"What is it?" Gassik asked.

Brunois just whistled under his breath, saying, "I no be sure what it is, but I do know I seen that there symbol before."

"Where?"

"With someone I don't care to talk with one bit. But I guess I'm gonna be havin' to."

CHAPTER

1

There sure be no place like home, Brunois thought as he stared out at the village. The sun had not long risen, and the grass was still wet. He could make out the sounds of life coming from the clusters of buildings. Livestock eager to be fed. Little ones eager to get out of doing such chores. An occasional peal of laughter as a greeting was exchanged. There sure was no place like home, and Brunois was sure glad there wasn't.

From where he crouched, he was certain no one could see him. The tall grasses and other leafy foliage hid his small form well. The idea had occurred to him it might be better to simply sneak in during the night and take what he sought, but there was no need to risk being shot. He knew his brother would gladly give him anything. After steeling himself another moment, he stepped out onto the road and began to walk into the village.

It had been many years since Brunois had set foot in his hometown. It didn't seem as if much had changed. The same dirt road, which led to the same stone bridge and let out onto the same village square. The pump handle on the well looked new, but that was about it.

He stood at the end of the bridge a moment and took everything in.

A few villagers walked about, many of who cast a glance at Brunois. His appearance was a bit disheveled, but he clearly was kin to the rest of the Frogs who lived here. Standing at five feet tall, Brunois Bonne'Chance was not a very imposing figure by most standards. His skin was a bright green, and he wore a navy blue double breasted jacket and off white trousers. Webbed feet were left bare, and much of his face was obscured by the wide brimmed hat he kept pulled forward. Most likely it was the revolvers he wore at each hip, and the sword slung across his back, that drew their attention. This was, after all, a peaceful place, inasmuch as it could be in this world.

Brunois began walking through the town toward the mill on the northern side. Memories stirred as he went—stealing a fresh loaf of bread from the baker, standing up on the low wall by the potter's store and having "swordfights" with carefully selected sticks for weapons. He stuffed such foolish memories down. There was no place for them in his life now.

As he walked by the church he stared at it. The steeple looked as if it loomed over this place, handing out judgment and condemnation in order to hold folks in their place. Brunois scoffed at it and laughed a little at the notion of a god and continued to walk toward his family's home.

The mill had been in his family for many generations. It was as old as the village itself, and indeed, the Bonne'Chance family had been one of the founders of Underbrook. The stone and timbers that formed its structure were massive, being two feet thick in some places. Attached to the side of it was a modest house with a red-tiled roof. He stepped through the doorway and croaked out, "Arcator! Ya here?"

A bright red girl of about fourteen came bounding out from the kitchen. Her expression was joyful when she laid eyes on the visitor. "Uncle Brunois!" she shouted as she ran up to him. "It's good to see you!"

Brunois smiled and nodded at the young Frog. "Aye. Good to be seein' ya too, Rana. Been a while."

Rana was the daughter of Arcator's wife, Estaire. Her first husband was a soldier who died defending their village from a warlord who had decided that their property should be his. Estaire had fled with Rana when the girl was but a few months old. Upon arriving in Underbrook, Arcator took them in and, in time, married Estaire and adopted Rana. The couple never had any children together, but Arcator genuinely loved Rana and raised her as his own.

"It's been five years! How come you don't visit more? It's so dreadfully boring around here. Daddy won't let me do anything or go anywhere."

"Well, ya know, I been busy. Is your dad about somewhere? I'd like to be speakin' wit 'em."

"Busy doing what? I would love to hear of all your adventures out in the world! Will you tell me? How long are you staying? Come, sit down and I'll fetch you some berries and you can tell me everything!"

Without waiting for a response, Rana turned and ran back into the kitchen, leaving Brunois standing in the main room of the house.

Boy, that girl got some spirit to her.

He croaked out a chuckle and called out to her, "Be best iffn' I just speak with your dad. Is he over in the mill?"

Rana returned with a bowl of blackberries, a pitcher of milk, cups, plates, spoons, and napkins all somehow balanced in her arms. Her face sunk at her uncle's refusal. She began to set the things down on the table, saying, "Yes. He's over in the mill."

Brunois gave a nod and a "Thank ya" and walked back out and around to the mill.

Arcator was busy grinding cornmeal when Brunois entered. The great stones turned steadily, powered by the waterwheel on the back of the structure. Arcator looked up from his work and smiled.

"Brunois! Welcome home!"

He set down the bag of corn and walked up to Brunois, embracing him. Brunois hugged him back the bare minimum.

"How have you been?" Arcator asked.

"I been well 'nough, Arcator. Yerself?"

His brother's face darkened as a look of deep sadness washed across it. "All right I suppose. Estaire passed away last winter. She caught a fever and just couldn't shake it. The doctor tried everything he could, but…"

Brunois shifted uncomfortably. He had liked Estaire well enough but didn't really know what to say to his brother, so he didn't say it. A silence, which was entirely too long for his liking, filled the space between them.

"Rana took it real hard, as you would expect a girl her age to," Arcator continued with a sigh. "But enough of sadness, this is a happy day that you've come to visit. Come, let's go into the house and get something to eat. I'll bet Rana will be happy to see you. How long can you stay with us?"

"Actually, I can no be stayin' long at all. I came to see iffn' ya still had some of Grandpop's old things. I was hopin' you might let me have one of 'em."

Arcator hid the hurt better than Rana had, but it was still there. He nodded. "Aye, I still have whatever of his he left. It's packed away in a trunk down in the root cellar. You're welcome to have whatever out of it you want. Are you sure you can't stay for at least the night? You hardly ever come to visit."

Brunois stared his brother in the eye for a long moment before shaking his head. "Ya know how it be Arc. Dad died when we was still kids. You was the one what stayed 'ere with mom and went to school and such. I went out on me own, and that be where I belong."

With a sigh and a nod, Arcator led Brunois back to the house. Rana sat at the table, her head propped up on one hand as she popped berries into her mouth.

"Rana, look who's come for a visit."

"Aye, he came in already."

She didn't even look up at him. Arcator just gave a nod and continued down to the root cellar.

Once there, he began to sort through a series of crates and trunks until he found the one he was looking for and drug it out.

"There it is then, whatever grandpop left is in there."

Brunois popped the latch open and began sorting through the contents. There was an old uniform of the

Royal Army decorated with several medals. Grandpop had been a brave soldier, defending Marlebonne from many a threat. As he shuffled things around, the creak of Rana's footsteps on the cellar stairs drew his attention.

"What are you looking for?" she asked.

Brunois turned to look at her. "Oh, nothin' really. Just an old trinket I seem to 'member Grandpop havin'."

"What do you want it for?"

No answer.

Rana turned to her dad. "You're just going to let him take it?"

Arcator shrugged. "It's just as much his as it is mine, and whatever it is, I certainly have no use for it."

"What if it's worth something?"

Another shrug. "He can have it. Like I said, it's just as much his as mine."

By this point, Rana had joined the pair by the trunk. Brunois continued to move the contents into the lid, searching for whatever prize he hoped to find. He found it inside a small wooden box. A grin spread across his Froggy face as he pulled it out and tucked it inside his jacket. He did the best he could to hide it from Rana, but she saw it anyway. It looked like some sort of key attached to a simple chain. She wondered what it was for.

Brunois placed the other items back in the trunk and shut the lid. He turned to Arcator. "Thanks then."

Arcator gave a nod. "That's it then? You sure you can't stay for just a meal?"

Brunois shook his head again. "Sorry, but be best iffn' I start makin' my way back to Ravenrock so I can catch the evenin' train."

Another nod from Arcator. "Aye then. Well, I guess it is still good to see you, however briefly." A pause. "You know, you are welcome here anytime. I do hope you can come back soon for a real visit.

"Aye. Perhaps."

The three Frogs walked back up from the cellar and into the house.

2

Brunois couldn't sit still while he waited for the train, so he paced the platform back and forth. He had practically flown back from Underbrook he was so excited, arriving several hours before the train was due. The platform's other occupant, a frumpy old Opossum, eyed him suspiciously and held tight to his bag.

A whistle blew in the distance. *Finally.* Brunois was so eager to return to Dunham that he was considering walking. The train came down the tracks and screeched to a halt, four painted cars behind a locomotive of steel and brass. Brunois presented his ticket, and after suffering an admonishment from the Rabbit conductor over his weapons, he boarded. He took a seat by the window and thought about what was to come.

His hand reached into his jacket, and he ran his thumb across the key, grinning as he felt the two wings that formed the top of it. What great fortune to have stumbled across something like this. There was no telling of all the riches he was going to find.

Before long, the train was on its way. Brunois leaned his head against the window and stared at the landscape as it passed by. The colors were stark from the setting sun. This was the land of the Fierchevals, the kingdom of Marlebonne. The noble family of Horses had ruled these lands since the time of the Rebirth, when some of the Wastes were turned back into habitable lands. They were generally well liked by the populace and considered to be fair and just rulers. It had been their resources that allowed for the construction of the railroad, and they also funded the Royal Academy, where artifacts of old were examined and new technologies developed.

Brunois's mind wandered as the hypnotic rhythm of the train on the track drew him toward sleep. He hadn't slept in over a day, having walked all night from Ravenrock to Underbrook and then turning and walking back. His feet were sore and his legs tired. The surge of excitement was being subsumed by exhaustion. Sleep won over.

Dreams were never sweet for Brunois. They were always haunted by familiar phantoms. Distorted faces frozen in tormented expressions howled noiselessly at him. There were men. There were women. There were children. A parade of nameless ghosts, chanting his name. He tried to run from them. He ran until his chest burned and his legs crumbled to dust. He ran until the road had turned to nothingness and only an empty expanse of space lay below him. He ran and ran and ran, but the ghastly procession assailed him still. Some things you just can't run away from.

The train jolted him awake with a sudden lurch. It took a moment for him to shake off the visions, but slowly, the interior of the car came back into focus. The train had come to a stop. A few shouts could be heard coming from the front. Brunois hopped out of his seat and crouched low, drawing and cocking his revolvers as he moved. He scanned the wooden paneling and leather-bound seats; the few passengers he shared the car with traded looks of concern and annoyance. A minute passed. Then two. Then three. Brunois began to contemplate breaking the window and escaping.

Finally, the conductor entered the car from the front. "No problems, folks, nothing to worry about. Seems there was just a stowaway, and when they got caught, they bumped the controls. We've gotten rid of them, and we'll be on our way again in a moment."

The other passengers in the car looked relieved, but Brunois was very uneasy. Too much of a coincidence. Brunois didn't like it. He sat back in his seat but kept his revolvers in his hands, although he did ease the hammers back down. The Opossum he had shared the platform with stared hard at him. Brunois glared back and the Opossum turned away. The train heaved forward and began its eastward trek again.

There would be no more sleep tonight. It didn't upset him too much. No sleep meant no dreams. While awake, he could push back the horrors that filled his memories, but while asleep, he was defenseless. He shook his head and forced himself to think of other things. He reached into his jacket again and felt the winged top of the key. The dread and pain were replaced with excitement.

The remainder of the ride to Dunham took until the morning. As the train pulled into the station, a crowd could be seen awaiting its arrival. Some of the constables stood on the platform, and there were more out in the street. They looked alert. The doors of the train opened, and the passengers began to disembark. Brunois hung back and watched the deputy constables. They were checking everyone as they exited.

Damn. He didn't think they had seen him through the window, so at least he had a few more moments. He made for the door that led to the next car back and slipped down under the train where the cars hitched together. From there, he crawled under the platform and waited. Once the train left and the crowd dispersed, the deputies would probably leave too. No sense in being stationed there if there wasn't a train due. He would just wait them out.

It took a full hour before the train was boarded, loaded, resupplied, and ready to go. Once it was, the street around the railway station began to empty as well. One by one, Brunois watched the guards return to other duties. He was just about to sneak out from his hiding place when he heard a familiar voice. A moment later, its familiar owner came bounding into view. *Damn.*

3

Rana decided she was going to follow Brunois before he had even left the house. Whatever that key opened, she wanted to know. She wanted to be there when it was opened. Life in this small town was so unbearably dull, and this was her chance for adventure. Her dad would never let her go though.

I'll have to sneak away.

After Brunois was out of sight, Arcator turned to Rana, plainly seeing that she was upset at her uncle's cold treatment of her. He offered a father's compassion, saying, "He can be a real cur sometimes. Sorry it was such a lousy visit for you."

Rana merely nodded and feigned a deep hurt. It wasn't too hard to do—she really was upset—but she did have to suppress the excitement beginning to well up within her. "It's fine," she said and let out a sigh. "He probably didn't have anything worth hearing anyways." She began to clear the table she had set only minutes before.

Arcator watched her for a moment. "Well, I should get back to my work. But how about when I finish for the morning, you and I go have a picnic out in the meadow for our lunch?"

A slight smile spread across Rana's face. "All right, that sounds nice. I'll start to fix us a basket then."

Arcator gave her a loving squeeze on the shoulder and then returned to the mill.

Rana flew into action, gathering all she would need for her journey. Or at least all she thought she would need. She got the canvas rucksack that she took to the market sometimes and filled it with an extra set of clothes, a few loaves of bread, and a tin bottle to be filled with water. She changed out of the dress she was wearing and into a pair of brown trousers and a white blouse, completing the outfit with a leather jacket and a white bandanna tied around her head. On the way out the door, she took a moment to squeeze the locket that hung around her neck. It had been a gift fom her father. *Sorry, but I can't say good-bye.*

Her dad, still at work in the mill, was oblivious to his daughter's departure. She slipped through the town, trying to remain unseen, lest a neighbor question her about her odd choice of dress and travel pack. A quick stop at the water pump to fill her bottle, and she was out of the village and on her way.

Despite her haste in making preparations, more than an hour had passed since Brunois had left for Ravenrock. And even if she could make up the time on the road, she couldn't risk him seeing her. She would have to take the paths through the woods. It was fortunate for her she knew them well.

There was a stream that ran toward Ravenrock, and she ambled along its banks. The thrill of adventure and the warm sun spurred her webbed footsteps. The forest celebrated with her. Soft breezes stirred the green foliage. A few stray butterflies danced about in the air. Woodland song and chatter drifted through the trees. She would be in Ravenrock in no time.

When she arrived, her heart sank to see Brunois already on the platform. *But what did you really expect?* She wasn't going to be able to buy a ticket and board without getting spotted. She would have to stow away.

The railroad station was on the edge of town. Rana hid in the woods and waited, watching her uncle pace back and forth on the platform.

She wondered what had him so excited. The key he had found in his grandfather's things was certainly at the center of it. Rana didn't know much about her adoptive great grandfather. Her father spoke of him sometimes, but she had never paid much attention to the stories. He may have been a soldier.

The train pulled up to the station. Rana watched her uncle and a frumpy-looking Opossum board it. Now was her chance. Crouching low, she took off for the train, trying to move in the long shadows cast by the setting sun. The train only had four cars plus the engine. She could choose between the two passenger cars, a baggage car, or the coal car. *Baggage car it is.* She clambered into it and found a place to hide among some of the crates.

The train let out a roar and began to move forward. Her heart raced as it picked up speed. She was on her way to adventure. She began to wonder if she had leapt without looking. *Probably.*

Rana had never been any further from home than Ravenrock. She had heard stories of what the rest of the world was like from the occasional traveling merchant. The castles of Chevaire, the towers of the Royal Academy, the Magisterium in Bakhtin, the horrors of the Wastes. Stories of those places had filled her with dreams of venturing out from the small village of Underbrook and making stories of her own. Now was her chance. As tired as she was, there would be no sleep for Rana this night. The excitement of the unknown, equal parts fear and hope, would not allow it.

When the back door to the car opened, Rana froze. She held her breath and did her best to creep noiselessly into the shadows, covering her red skin with her jacket to better cloak her presence. The conductor walked down the center of the car, a lantern in hand. His nose twitched, and the long Rabbit ears that hung down from his hat moved a bit. He came to a sudden halt and stared along the length of the car.

"Who's there?" he called out into the darkness.

Rana bit her lip and hugged her knees tight to her chest.

The conductor began to search in between the rows of crates. One at a time, he moved from stack to stack. Rana's heart thumped so hard in her chest she was certain he would hear it. She knew she would be discovered, so she jumped out from her hiding place and bolted for the door out into the night.

"Stop!"

Once out of the car, she hopped up onto the ladder of the coal car and began running across the roof of it. Or at least trying to, with the train moving so fast, it was more of a rapid crawl. When she reached the other side, she dropped down in between the coal car and the locomotive.

Now what?

With no other choice, she opened the door and ducked into the cab of the locomotive, much to the surprise of the engineer. The Fox at the controls started at her intrusion and hollered "Who are you?" as he reached for something to defend himself with.

"I, um, I am…I'm not looking for trouble," Rana stammered. "Please, just keep quiet…I, uh…"

Her babbling was cut off by the appearance of the conductor, who now held a pistol in his hand. He pointed it at Rana. She gulped. "Now then, miss, just what are you doing here?"

"I, uh, was…um…I was…" Rana began to shake. So did the engine. The conductor and the engineer looked around nervously. Rana tried to hold back, but there was no stopping it. Steam burst out of one valve, then another. The train heaved and began to slow down as the pressure dropped. The engineer was thrown up against the wall, and the conductor knocked off his feet.

Rana remained hunched toward the side of the cabin. Her expression was pinched. "Sorry…" she croaked out. "I didn't mean to. That kind of thing happens when I get upset."

The two men stared at one another a moment. The conductor spoke up, "Who are you, miss?"

"My name is Rana. Rana Pimienta." She gave her birth name. It seemed right. "I, uh, I needed to get to Dunham, but I didn't have any money for a ticket. My father died, and I didn't have anywhere else to go. I have an aunt there. I was hoping to go live with her." She was a little surprised with the ease at which she lied, but she didn't want to let on anything about her true purpose or her relation to one of the passengers.

Another look passed between the two men. This time, it was the engineer who spoke, asking, "Are you a sorceress, miss?"

This wasn't the first time she had been asked that. There had been several times throughout her life when this sort of thing had happened. She had tried to stuff it down, tried to control it, but it always came out sooner or later.

"Well, I'm not really sure…" she answered.

The conductor retrieved his revolver from where it had fallen and, after considering it for a moment, he replaced it in its holster under his jacket. The engineer looked over at him. "Jack, she's just a kid. Let's give her a ride. We can't just leave her out here in the middle of the night."

The Rabbit frowned a moment then nodded reluctantly. "All right. Fine. But she stays up here with you and Chouk. I don't want the other passengers being disturbed. I'll go and calm them down. Just get us back underway."

The two men nodded at one another, and Jack the Rabbit exited the locomotive. The Fox engineer walked over to Rana and offered his paw. "Name's Kelvin, miss. Pleased to meet you." She accepted his paw and stood up.

"Ol' Jack's a nice enough fellow, just takes his job real serious," Kelvin continued. "You all right?"

Rana nodded. He nodded back.

"Right then. Let's take a look at the damage." Kelvin went over to the valves and began inspecting them.

"Ah, this ain't so bad, they just got a little over loaded. Too much pressure. A quick patch should do until we get to Dunham and I can get replacements." He turned to the rear of the locomotive and hollered, "Chouk! Get the toolbox!"

A moment later, a Mole wearing stained and dusty overalls appeared, toolbox in hand. He looked as if he lived in the coal car. "What happened? I was gettin' a load when I hear all this crazy hollerin', and then the train come to a stop…."

Kelvin nodded over to Rana. "We've got ourselves a guest. Rana, meet Chouk. He's my fireman."

Chouk did not look happy with that answer.

"Fireman?" Rana asked, eyeing the Mole suspiciously.

"Aye, fireman. He shovels coal for me, keeps the boiler going. Now then, let's see…" He took the toolbox from Chouk and began searching through it. "I keep some cinnamon candies in a box up at the controls if you want one," he said to Rana without turning from his work.

She walked over and got one, popping it into her mouth with a weak smile. "Thanks," she replied and sat down with her back to the wall.

It wasn't long before Kelvin and Chouk finished their repairs and started the train moving again. He looked down at her with compassionate eyes. "We should be in Dunham by the morning, little miss. Why don't you try and get some sleep."

Rana nodded, but there would be no sleep for her. The train chugged on.

4

What is she doing here? Brunois asked himself as he watched Rana walk down the street. *And how did she get here?*

It was obvious that she had followed him, but whatever possessed her to do such a thing was beyond his reckoning. *No matter.* He had waited out the deputies; he would just wait her out too. So he waited. A full hour. And she was still there. He decided that he would try and sneak by her.

Once her back was turned, he scrambled out from under the platform and began to walk down the street away from her. He was almost at the corner when he heard her call out, "Uncle Brunois!"

He cursed under his breath and kept walking, attempting to disappear into the city. He heard his name shouted again. Seems he would have to entertain her a moment after all, just so she would stop shouting his name. Once she had him in clear view, he ducked down a side street so their conversation would be somewhat private.

Back against the wall, hat pulled over his face, he waited for her to round the corner. When she did she almost walked right past him.

"What'chya doin' here, Rana?"

Her eyes were aflame as she turned on him. "Looking for you."

"Here I am. Now what?"

Her eyes narrowed into a glare, her mouth into a pout. "What did you want that key for?"

"That no be any bus'ness o' yers."

"It is now. I want to know." Her expression softened a little. "I want to come with you. I want to have an adventure." A slight smile crossed her mouth with the word "adventure."

Brunois croaked out a scoff. "I don't know what'ya think I be doin', but the world ain't like ya heard in some fairy tale. It ain't a bunch o' heroes flyin' 'bout savin' damsels in distress."

"I still want to know why you wanted that key."

"And that still no be any bus'ness o' yers."

Rana's glare became intense.

"Hey! I have just as much a right to it as you!"

"No ya' don't. Yer not a blood relation."

She really lost it with that comment. "How dare you!" She screamed, jabbing a finger at him to accentuate her point. A small flame shot from her hand with the motion.

With a croak of surprise, Brunois hopped out of the way. The tiny fireball scorched the brick wall he had been leaning against. Silence reigned between them as they both tried to think of something to say.

It was Brunois who finally asked, "How did'ya be doin' that?"

Rana blushed—that is, her cheeks turned a deeper shade of red than they already were, and she bowed her head a little. "I'm not really sure. That sort of thing just happens sometimes when I'm upset."

"Can ya control it?"

A shake of the head. "No, not really. Not well, at least."

"But iffn' ya get angry enough it just happen?"

"Angry or scared. Yeah, pretty much."

"How big can ya be makin' it?"

Rana smiled. So it seemed they now wanted something from each other. "Why so interested?"

Brunois grinned. *Maybe she be smarter than she looks. Maybe.* He shrugged. "Just wonderin' is all."

They stared at each other a moment.

"Tell ya what," Brunois said, "ya can come 'long with me to see what I wanted the key fer. But ya gotta be doin' just as I say you do, aye?"

Rana's smile was so broad and bright Brunois thought she was going to combust. "Yes! Aye! Absolutely! Thank you!" She crashed into her uncle, hugging him tightly.

He croaked uncomfortably and extricated himself from her clutch.

"Right. Be no need fer all that then."

Without saying anything else, he checked the street for any constables or deputies and then stepped back out, walking at a brisk pace. Rana kept up.

The streets of Dunham were crowded. It was a busy trading hub, and the main one on the eastern side of the kingdom. As the pair of Frogs walked through the streets, Rana couldn't help but stare at some of the sights. Fancy clothes, exotic foods, strange Animals speaking strange languages. There were so many different smells and sounds, all intermingling in a way that made it difficult for her to distinguish one from the other. She happily drank in all the activity but tried to hide her awe.

They walked for almost two hours before reaching their destination. It was in a part of the city that made Rana uncomfortable. The streets were far dirtier than the other parts they had walked through. So were the Animals. Many of them looked sick, and the ones that didn't looked predatory. A few of them even called out to her in names she had never heard before but caught their meaning well enough. She looked up at Brunois, who had hardly said a word to her since they began walking.

"So…is this it?"

"Aye, it is," he said and pushed open the door to a small pawnbroker's shop. A Rat was behind the counter wearing a white shirt with a gray waistcoat. He had a number of golden rings on his fingers and was inspecting another with a jeweler's loupe when they entered.

Brunois croaked out, "Ho there, Gassik."

The Rat looked up and nodded, his eyes sweeping over Rana. "Who's the girl?"

"No one. Don't be worryin' about it."

"I worry about everything."

Brunois stared at the Rat a long moment before laughing under his breath. "She be my niece. Her name's Rana."

"Niece? Never had you figured for the sentimental sort."

"You never had me figured at all."

A shrill squeak of laughter came from the Rat. "Think what you want. I know ya better than you know yourself."

Brunois walked up to the counter and retrieved the key with the winged top from his jacket, setting it on the counter. Gassik stared at it a moment. After pursing his mouth and eyeing it, he disappeared into the back of the shop, returning a moment later. He placed a metal object resembling an egg the size of a melon next to the key.

Rana, who had been hanging back behind her uncle, walked up to the counter and stared at the egg. She had never seen anything like it. It was made from some sort of shiny metal. Six seams ran lengthwise from the narrow end to the wide end, dividing it into leaves of a sort. There was a golden pattern in low relief around the wide end, forming a stand that allowed the egg to sit with the narrow end pointing upward. At the top was a small hole where the leaves all came together, and in the center of each leaf was a symbol etched into the metal of two insectile wings flanking an oval. The same symbol was on the top of the key.

A smile bloomed on Rana's face as she blurted out, "The key is for this!"

The Rat and the Frog both glanced at her, their amusement plain. Rana blushed, embarrassed by her outburst. The three of them stared at the two objects.

"Guess I'll be doin' the honors then," Brunois said, picking up the key.

He had to stand on his toes in order to reach the top of the egg. The key slid inside the hole smoothly.

Brunois turned it, feeling a bit of resistance, like winding a clock. He shot a glance at the other two and then continued to wind. After many turns, the tension came to the point of stopping. He withdrew the key.

With a click and a whir the leaves began to bloom outward. The trio watched in awe as the device blossomed from egg to flower. The inside of each leaf was lined with brightly colored metals of purple and green. At the center was a golden sphere that was also beginning to open. Everyone went wide-eyed with amazement as what appeared to be an insect made of brass was revealed.

It resembled a firefly in its construction. The body was oval in shape, with two sets of wings lying along its back and three sets of legs along its length. Two large eyes made of some type of amber gem dominated its head, and another large piece of amber was at its rear. In the center of its back, between the wings, was a small hole.

Brunois eyed the key he still held in his hand. It didn't appear as if it would fit in the mechanical firefly's back, but he tried anyway. It did not.

He let out a croak of disappointment, "Damn."

Rana frowned, and Gassik hissed in annoyance.

"May I see the key?" Rana asked Brunois.

He took a moment before nodding and handing it over. Rana studied it closely. It looked as if there might be a seam where the blade met the bow. She grasped each firmly and twisted in opposite directions. There was a faint click, and the blade came away, revealing a smaller one beneath.

Rana beamed at her discovery. Brunois's eyes
became large and he held out his hand for the return of
the key. Reluctantly, and with a hurt look, Rana relin-
quished the key to Brunois, who turned back to the
metallic insect. The key fit perfectly. He turned it a single full turn.

The eyes of the firefly flickered with light and its
wings began to beat. Slowly it rose from the tiny pedestal on which it sat within the now open flower, the key
turning in its back. Brunois stared directly into its eyes,
and it stared right back at him.

None of them had even realized their mouths had
dropped open. They all simply beheld the tiny brass
spectacle as it hovered in Gassik's rundown pawn shop.
The light on its rear flashed several times, and then it
simply ceased to move and fell unceremoniously onto
the counter.

Brunois absently muttered something that sounded
like it had the word "God" in it. Gassik and Rana both
uttered equally inarticulate statements. A long silence
sat in the middle of the three of them, centered on the
mechanical insect.

Gassik turned to Brunois and asked, "Where did
you get this again?"

"From a Dog what thought I had some o'his money."

"I see. And where did he get it?"

"I don't know, but I means to be findin' out. You know
anyone what be knowledgeable 'bout things like this?"

Gassik began to shake his head and then reconsid-
ered. "There is one that I think might know something
in regards to this."

"You think ya can set up a meetin' with him?"

A laugh from the Rat. "Her. And yes. But…"

"But what?"

"She'll probably want to go with you."

Rana perked up at that last statement from Gassik. "You're going to go out on an adventure then? Can I come with you?" Rana realized she had asked a question and quickly changed it to, "I'm coming with you!"

Brunois just gave a short nod and picked the firefly up from where it lay.

"Iffn' ya want to be comin', Rana, then you got to be lookin' out fer yerself. I no am gonna be yer nursemaid, ya gotta pull yer own weight, aye?"

Rana hopped about.

"Yes! Yes! I'll pull my weight! Thank you!"

Brunois turned back to Gassik, asking, "You think ya can set this meetin' up fer tomorrow?"

"I can try."

"We be gettin' a room nearby then. I'll check back in th'morning and see what be what."

Brunois put the firefly in his jacket, along with the key, and walked out the door. Rana glided along behind him, her excitement warming the air around her.

CHAPTER

5

"Where am I supposed to sleep?"

Rana was not happy. The room only had one bed, and Brunois had already plopped down on it. He had pulled his hat over his face and was doing a good job of ignoring her.

"Well?" Her face was becoming even redder than its natural hue, which was quite bright to begin with.

From beneath his hat, Brunois croaked out, "Floor."

"You can't expect me to really sleep on the floor? It's filthy! This place looks like it hasn't been cleaned in ages!"

She wasn't wrong. The dingy lodging Brunois had obtained for the night was a seedy place not far from the docks. The air was thick with the smells of tar and disease. The wooden floor and walls were warped and had rat holes, the common rats that occupied them plainly seen.

"Yer free to get yer own room elsewhere iffn'ya want."

Rana grew silent.

"But I haven't much money...."

Brunois scoffed a bit. The hat didn't do much to muffle it.

"Shoulda brought more then."

"Can I at least have one of the blankets?"

Silence.

"Please?" Rana sounded as if she might start crying.

"Fine."

Brunois rolled off the bed and yanked one of the blankets out, tossing it at Rana without looking at her, then lying back down.

Rana smiled a little and said, "Thanks." It was weakly said, but she was beginning to realize she didn't know as much as she thought she did. She arranged her rucksack as a pillow and curled up within the blanket.

"Uncle Brunois?"

"Don't be callin' me uncle. Brunois be fine."

"Brunois?"

"What?"

"Why haven't you wound the bug up again?"

"Why would I care to?"

"Don't you wonder what else it can do?"

"Not really."

"I do."

Silence.

"I'll bet it can do all sorts of other things. Do you think it has thoughts? Or feelings?"

"Why would I care iffn' it be havin' thoughts or feelin's? It be a metal bug. It's just a thing I goin' to be sellin' when I be havin' the right chance and right price."

"You really don't care what else it does?"

"Not even a little."

Rana sighed. The floor was hard and cold and the blanket didn't do much to alleviate either of those conditions. She found herself missing the comforts of home. *I guess if it wasn't hard, it wouldn't be an adventure.* That thought, while nice, didn't alleviate the cold hard floor either.

"Unc…er, uh, Brunois?"

Brunois sighed. "What?"

"Why don't you get along with my dad?"

"We get along just fine."

"Then why don't you come to visit more?"

"Got me better things to do."

"Like what?"

"Like none o' yer business."

"Like treasure hunting?"

"Sometimes."

"I'll bet you have lots of adventures."

"The world ain't some story waitin' t'happen, Rana. It be a hard place what kill ya."

"That's why you need me. To watch your back."

"I don't be needin' ya, Rana."

"Oh, sure you do. You just don't know it yet."

As much as he hated her incessant talking, he had to laugh a little at her spirit.

"Besides, everyone needs someone," Rana continued.

"Not me."

"You have no one you would call a friend? What about that Rat?"

"Gassik? You no wanna let him fool you. He ain't nobody's friend. He'd sell us out in a second for scant more than pocket change."

"So you have no one in your life?"

"There be lots o' folks in my life."

"But no one special?"

"No one but m'self."

"Why?"

"Because folks be awful at the core."

"Not everyone."

"Most everyone."

"Even me?"

A pause.

"Yer comin' dangerously close to it."

Rana smiled. Her heart warmed.

"Good night, Uncle Brunois."

"I said don't call me uncle."

"I know."

6

Morning couldn't come soon enough for Rana. Between the appalling lodgings and the scores of rats she had shared them with, she had barely slept at all. When Brunois had finally woken, she was all too eager to be up and out of the squalid place. The pair of Frogs left the inn and walked back to Gassik's shop.

Brunois stopped on the way and bought something to eat from a Gopher at a small food cart. Rana ate some of the food she had brought with her as they walked. Not many words passed between them as they went through the awakening streets. The walk was not overly long, and both of them were just finishing their simple breakfasts as they arrived.

There was already someone inside speaking with Gassik. She was a Horse with bright coppery ringlets and a spotted roan coat. Her posture was tall and proud. An elegant bow was slung across her back, and she wore a simple green vest over a plain white blouse, and matching green short pants.

Brunois walked in with Rana trailing close behind. Gassik saw their entrance and called over to them,

"Brunois! Rana! Come on over here. This is the one I was telling you about."

The woman turned to face the approaching Frogs. She nodded and smiled. It was warm and sincere. "Pleased to meet you, Brunois, Rana. My name is Auroka."

Brunois nodded his greeting. Rana was a bit more exuberant and burst out with, "Pleased to meet you too!"

Brunois and Gassik exchanged a glance. It was Gassik who spoke up, reaching under the counter as he did so, "Now then, the reason I asked you here is to take a look at this." Gassik set the egg on the counter. It was closed back up to its original state.

Auroka raised her eyebrows and nodded a little. "A rare treasure," she said as she bent down to examine it closer. "What was inside it?"

"What makes ya think there was somethin' inside it?" Brunois asked, his eyes narrowing a bit with the question.

Auroka didn't look up from her inspection but answered, "This has been opened recently and the only reason that you would close it back up is that you found something in it but wished not to let on you did."

Brunois croaked out a chuckle. He reached in his jacket and took out the mechanical firefly, holding it up and saying, "This bug here was inside it."

Auroka straightened up to look at the curious clockwork insect. Her eyes became wide when she saw it. She held out her hand and asked, "May I hold it?"

Brunois carefully handed it over to Auroka, who held it close to her face and examined every aspect of it.

"How amazing…." She mused. "Do you have the key to wind it?"

Brunois nodded and croaked out, "I do."

Auroka handed it back to him, "Would you mind showing me?"

With one hand, he took the firefly, and with the other, he reached inside his jacket for the key. He placed the firefly on the counter and wound it two turns. It sprung to life with a flicker of its eyes and a beating of its wings then rose straight into the air. It stared at Brunois a moment before making a quick circle around the shop and landing on his shoulder and flashing the light on its tail end.

All four of them gasped. Brunois spasmed and he swatted the thing off his shoulder onto the floor. He immediately cursed his reaction and bent down to inspect it, hoping it remained undamaged. Fortunately, it was, and Brunois picked it up, removed the key from its back and placed it on the counter.

"Simply astounding," Auroka said, stooping forward once again to study it. "I have never seen such a thing as this. But these symbols"—she turned to the egg and pointed at the symbol etched on the leaves—"I have seen them before."

Brunois remained reserved, but Rana couldn't contain her words.

"Really? Where? Can you take us there? Is it far?"

Auroka laughed warmly, saying, "Easy now, little one. Calm yourself." She looked between the three others in the shop and said, "I have seen this symbol before, on doorways out by the edge of the Wastes. I believe them to be remnants of Svargan civilization. They are less than two weeks' journey to the east." She narrowed her eyes. "Where did you find this?"

"It more found me. Got it from a fellow at a game o' cards."

Auroka nodded slightly, not wholly believing that answer despite the straight face with which Brunois had offered it.

"Was the key with it?"

Brunois shook his head. "Nah. As luck would be havin' it, that be a family heirloom."

An expression of mild amusement washed over Auroka's face. "Perhaps it was fate then."

Brunois scoffed. "Be no such thing. This place, where ya say ya seen the symbol b'fore, think there be more o' these? Or somethin' else what this key might work fer?"

She shrugged. "It is possible. I have not explored the place too thoroughly nor, to my knowledge, has anyone else. It is not shown on any map that I am aware of." She stopped and thought a moment before adding, "It is indeed a question I would be most interested in having answered."

Brunois looked hard at Auroka. She was definitely the strong sort and obviously knew how to take care of herself. But there was something else about her, a certain air of nobility that lent forcefulness to her warmth.

She stared right back at him, forming her own opinions of the Frog. He seemed on the surface to be just another rogue, but the young girl with him seemed too naïve to be a partner in any way. That made her friend or family, which made Auroka think that perhaps there could be more to him than just what he chose to present himself as.

The two of them made up their minds and nodded to one another. Rana looked back and forth between them, not comprehending what was going on, but she did understand it when Brunois asked, "Can ya be ready by th'afternoon to depart then?"

Auroka nodded.

Rana hopped up and down excitedly and croaked out a "Yay!"

Everyone else rolled their eyes.

"Have you any experience out in the Wastes?" Auroka directed the question at Brunois, already knowing the answer she would get from Rana.

He nodded, saying, "Far more than I should be carin' to have."

"I'll go to gather my supplies then. Shall we meet at the East Gate later then? Two o'clock?"

Brunois nodded a bit and said, "Two o'clock be fine, but I'd rather leave the city in more discreet a fashion than just walkin' out o' the gate. Let's be meetin' at that little tavern three blocks in from the gate, and we can take another way out."

Auroka smirked but agreed.

"I think I should hold onto the egg then," Gassik said. "Don't think you folks will need it on the trail, and I'm certainly due something for my hand in arranging all of this." He returned the egg to behind the counter and out of sight before continuing, "And whatever you find out there, you should bring back here first. I can help you line up buyers for that sort of thing. Svargan relics aren't to just be sold to anyone, you need to have the right connections, know the right circles to be able to sell them."

Both Frogs and the Horse shot a wry look at Gassik, who simply maintained his self-important façade.

"We'll be seein' 'bout that, Gassik. But fer now, aye, ya can be keepin' the egg." Brunois collected the firefly and turned to Auroka. "Two o'clock then?"

She nodded and gave a slight bow to the others. "I shall see you then," she said, and walked out of the store.

The Frogs said their good-byes to Gassik and left to go gather supplies.

Gassik smiled and thought about how much he could sell the egg for. He bet he would get a lot for it.

7

Auroka waited patiently at the Roving Hound Tavern. She disliked the name. She disliked most Dogs in fact. Not so much as a Species, but most of them that she had ever met just seemed so awfully crass. She was glad that, despite the name, there were not many there to share the room with her. The tavern itself was a modest structure, made of simple wood and brick. It definitely did not cater to more refined tastes, but it was a respectable-enough establishment. At least the glass her water had come in was clean.

That was something.

Brunois and Rana came in a little before two o'clock, Brunois walking slowly enough to observe his surroundings as he went, Rana almost tripping over her own webbed feet she was so excited. Auroka laughed to herself at the exuberance of youth, an act that was immediately followed by the hope that the little red Frog would not get them all killed while out in the Wastes. She stood to greet the pair.

"Hello again, sir and miss."

Brunois tipped his hat and croaked out a "ma'am," but Rana shouted, "Hi!"

The elder Frog rolled his eyes and asked, "All set then?"

Auroka nodded and picked a pack up off the floor. She noted the packs her new partners were carrying. They seemed to be an adequate size to contain the supplies they would need. She debated checking to see what they had brought but decided Brunois had enough experience to know what was needed and would probably be insulted if she asked. "All set," she said, and slung the pack across her back, and then her bow in the other direction.

Brunois raised an eyebrow at her. "No arrows?"

"No need."

He kept the eyebrow raised for a moment before nodding and walking to the exit.

As the three went out into the street, Brunois quickly turned and began walking southward, trying to conceal himself behind things without making it too obvious he was doing it, not that he had much trouble being unseen. The streets were always crowded in the early afternoon with traders and other such business-minded folk, especially this close to the gate. The stones of the streets chattered with steps of hoof, foot, and paw alike as everyone went about their affairs.

Auroka immediately saw the source of Brunois's desire to go unseen. Inspector Wourinos was standing by the yellow stone of the East Gate. The Badger was an imposing figure, despite being only average height at best. His dark-gray fur and black striped face made him look as if he had been chiseled out of a block of stone. The stoic expression he wore confirmed this thought. The inspector was not someone Auroka had much desire to hold a conversation with, so she was content to follow Brunois through his meandering route toward the city outskirts.

Rana was not as perceptive. "What's going on? Why are we going this way?"

Brunois kept his head turned away but answered, "Just be the best way to be goin' to get out o' the city without bein' spotted."

"Spotted by who?" Rana asked, trying to keep her breath as she raced to keep up with Brunois and Auroka.

"The inspector, or any o' his constables."

Any further questions would have to wait as the three ducked down an alley and had to navigate some discarded crates and other refuse. Auroka bounded over the obstacles easily, allowing Brunois to lead the way. Rana struggled to keep up but was determined not to call out. She had said she would pull her own weight, and she meant to do just that—no matter how hard it was.

She couldn't quite tell what direction they were headed; the maze of alleys and side streets disoriented her, especially at the speed they were traversing them. Rana had to keep looking back and forth between Brunois and the ground just to ensure she did not fall face-first onto the road. She almost tripped several times and had earned a look from the other two as she croaked out a high-pitched cry.

Another quick turn, another stretch of navigating discarded rubbish, and another slipping through what looked like someone's private property, and they were upon a small wrought iron gate in a fieldstone wall.

Brunois popped the latch, opened the gate, and ushered the other two through, scanning the surroundings a final time before ducking out himself.

He turned to find Auroka standing calmly, and Rana with her hands on her knees, breathing heavily. Rana could feel his annoyance, like a burning sensation, as he stared at her. She forced herself to stand upright and tried to even out her breath. She was not too successful in either endeavor.

Auroka, seeing that Rana needed a moment, looked over to Brunois and asked, "How is it you know the inspector? If you don't mind me asking, that is."

Brunois shrugged and replied, "Him and I have had words b'fore 'bout stuff. Most times, we don't be agreein'. This time, though, I feel like I might get blamed fer a good bit that was no my fault." He gave Auroka a look—a knowing look. "How d'you know him then? I saw ya recognize 'em once I made 'em."

"He's a friend of my family."

"And you no be gettin' along with him?"

Auroka shrugged a little. "He's a good friend of my father's. Neither of them thinks I should make my own choices in life but rather just do as they say."

Brunois nodded, not believing that to be the whole of the story, but also not particularly caring for the details of it either. "We be gettin' on our way then?"

He looked over to Rana, who was once again bent over with her hands on her knees.

"Rana," he said.

She got angry that he wasn't asking her a question but rather telling her that she needed to pull it together.

Still, not much she could do about it, so she straightened up. She did her best to signal she was ready to
continue onward; it consisted of slightly leaning her
head forward while she panted for air. It was enough
for Brunois.

"Well, from 'ere it be yer way to go, miss. So which
way? We be on the eastern side o' Dunham."

Auroka looked at Rana and waited for her to regain
her breath. When it finally happened, she turned and
walked eastward, waving the two Frogs on behind her.

CHAPTER

8

"Ya certain it be the same one ya lost?" The big Dog's voice was harsh as he barked out the question.

"Yeah, boss, it be the same. That Rat must've gotten it from the Frog what took it from us," the smaller Dog replied, his tail tucked firmly between his legs.

Rache nodded. He was an imposing figure, tall and muscular, with black fur that looked shiny and well-groomed. Steel-gray eyes and bone-white teeth made his face truly frightening.

"Yer lucky to have found it. Lucky I let ya live long 'nough to find it."

Rache strode through the door of Gassik's shop and looked the Rat square in the eye. To Gassik's credit, he did not simply wilt under the force of the stare but instead asked, "May I help you?"

"Yeah, I do be believin' ya can." There was a dull thud as Rache set his paws on the glass display case.

"That there egg"—Rache nodded to the silver and golden egg in the display case—"it be mine. Was stolen from one o' my lads by a Frog I think ya know. I be wil-lin' to believe ya didn't know that so if you just hand it over, we can be done here." The words were said with a grin the anticipated outcome all too apparent.

Gassik was not to be bullied. He hadn't owned a pawn shop by the docks for so many years by being a pushover. He stared back at Rache, saying, "I'd be more than happy to sell it to you for a fine price. A rare treasure like this is quite valuable, as I'm sure you know, but I'd be willing to let it go for, say, five hundred?"

A snarl distorted Rache's face, and a growl left his throat. He swept a jewelry box off the countertop, staring at Gassik the whole time. By this point, there were four other Dogs in the store, with one of them standing right in front of the door and another in front of the large window. Gassik gulped.

"Open the case up, Rat," Rache growled.

"No. It's mine, fair and square."

Rache reached over the counter and picked Gassik up by his coat, pulling him halfway over so they were muzzle to snout.

"Maybe I'll just break it open with yer head then."

"Wait!" the Rat squealed. "What if I told you they were going out to find more of these? They have a guide who can take them to an uncharted Svargan ruin. I could tell you where to find them."

Rache pondered the offer a moment. "How do I know ya not just tell me some fool story to be rid o' me? You don't seem like the truthful sort."

Gassik wriggled a bit to avoid being strangled by his own collar. He was beginning to wheeze as he said, "Why would I lie? You would know where to find me."

Rache seemed to accept this answer, although he held fast to Gassik. "Where did they be goin' then?"

"East. Out of the East Gate or thereabouts. You shouldn't have trouble picking up their scent. They have a girl with them. Can't be more than fifteen."

"Who else be there?"

"Just the two Frogs, and a Horse. Auroka. She's the guide. A tough one, but nothing you and your boys couldn't handle."

Rache pulled the Rat the rest of the way over the counter and set him down, making a mock show of straightening out his clothes and dusting him off. He smiled at the Rat, saying, "Well then, that just be leavin' the matter of you openin' up this here case so I can get m'egg back."

"Wait, I thought we had a deal, I tell you where they went…"

Crash.

Midway through Gassik's protest, Rache's hefty paw grabbed the side of the Rat's head and smashed it into the display counter. Glass went everywhere, and Gassik went unconscious. The rest of the Dogs laughed. Rache bent down and retrieved the egg from the case.

It did have something strange to it, and Gassik had certainly been scared enough to tell the truth. *Maybe there do be more o' this sort out there,* Rache wondered.

He handed the egg to one of his Dogs and barked out, "Here, be storin' it somewhere's what's safe this time, or I be guttin' ya." He walked back out of the store, and the rest of the pack followed.

"Let's go see if we can't be findin' their trail at least."

The rest of the Dogs loped along behind their leader as he walked eastward. They joked and barked with one another as they went. Or at least until a look from Rache silenced their buffoonery.

Rache himself was deep in thought, an experience he was quite certain none of them had ever had nor were ever likely to. He knew that name, Auroka. She was rumored to have some sort of military training but chose to spend her time out in the wilds. And Brunois. This wasn't the first time that damned Frog had gotten in his way. *But it'll be the last, fer certain*, Rache growled to himself. Anger was always comforting. It made the revenge all the sweeter.

Inspector Wourinos was at the East Gate when they arrived. While Rache didn't have anything in particular to be worried about, he still preferred to avoid the Badger. He led his pack down a side street, but it was too late.

Two deputy constables, a Goat and a Bull the size of a small house, rounded the far corner and halted the Dogs. Snarls and growls were just beginning when Inspector Wourinos walked into the center of it all.

"Rache. just the one I was looking for. How are you today?"

"Just fine. Ya just here to talk or do you be wantin' somethin'?"

Wourinos frowned and asked, "Found one of yer boys the other night. Shot in the chest."

"Is that so? What make ya be thinkin' he be one o' mine?"

"He's a known associate of yours. We've seen him with you before."

"Got me all my associates right here," Rache replied, waving his arm to indicate the four Dogs that were with him.

"Oh, is that so? Still, I'd like you to come down to the morgue and take a look, see if you can identify the body. Your boys can come too."

Rache stared at the inspector for a long moment before saying, "Like I said, he can no be one o' mine since we all be here. Now if ya don't mind, we need to be on our way."

"On your way where?"

"We got some business. Outside o' the city."

"Why didn't you just go out of the gate then?"

"Duggar here forgot somethin'. Right, Duggar?"

One of the Dogs began to nod, stammering out, "Uh, yeah. I forgot my, uh, glasses. Have to go back to our rooms and see if the maid found 'em."

"Glasses, you say?" Wourinos looked long and hard at each of them.

"Yeah. Forgot his glasses, we was loopin' back fer 'em."

The silence that fell was heavy. So was Wourinos's stare as he leveled it at each Dog in turn.

"All right then, be on your way."

Wourinos and his deputy constables began walking back toward the East Gate. Rache and his Dogs continued south toward a side exit. Neither of them was happy about how that had gone.

After some maneuvering, the pack of Dogs wound their way outside the walls of Dunham and began searching for signs of their quarry's trail. It wasn't long before they found a few webbed footprints along with a set of hoofprints.

A grin crept across Rache's face again. *Vengeance indeed.*

CHAPTER

9

Rana had set out on this adventure full of excitement. Eight days of trudging through dense woods and rocky chasms, in weather that was alternately blistering hot and bone numbing cold, had done much to dampen that excitement. She was trying to remain positive in the face of such hardships, but it was tough.

Each night when they made camp, she struggled to perform the duties she had been assigned. She would collect stones and wood with which to build a fire and pile them up in the way Auroka had shown her. At least she proved her worth when it came time to light the fire. It often took her several tries, but she would eventually conjure enough flame to ignite the wood.

Once the fire had been lit, she would wrap herself in her blanket and begin to eat what food she had. She hadn't brought much, but Auroka would point out various plants as they walked that were edible, if not especially tasty. She was very grateful for the Horse's help. It was more than she was getting from her uncle.

Her feet were becoming increasingly sore. They were not used to such hard terrain and extended hiking. At night when they would rest, she would rub them for a little while, massaging the pain out of them. It helped some, but there were always more cuts and scrapes than the night before.

Brunois watched her faltering progress as she struggled to keep up. Maybe he had been wrong, after all, to allow her along. Fire or not, she was still just a kid and had no experience out in the world. Of course, neither had he when he set out from home at an even younger age than she. *Her choice to make. Anything bad happen to her, it be her own fault. Just hope she don't get me killed too.*

Auroka led the way with ease, the lands being very familiar to her. While there were roads that could be taken for much of the journey, she opted to lead them through rougher country. As one got further from civilization, the roads became more and more dangerous.

As they sat around the fire on the eighth night, Auroka informed them that they would reach a remote trader's outpost by sunset the following day.

"We should be able to resupply ourselves there," the Horse said.

Rana was busy rubbing her feet but managed to ask, "And from there, how far to the ruins?"

Brunois nodded his interest in that question and croaked out, "Aye, how much further then?"

"Another full day," Auroka said, looking at each Frog in turn.

Brunois tilted his head and asked, "How is it th'ruins be so close to an outpost like that and no one else ever be findin' 'em?"

"It's not really too surprising. The lands so close to the Wastes aren't too thoroughly explored. And the ruins themselves aren't very visible until you are right up on them."

"Ya mean they no be all that big?" he asked.

"Oh, I think they are very big, it's just that they are mostly underground. That's why I never explored them too much myself."

Rana glanced up from tending to her feet and stared at Auroka, mumbling, "Underground?"

Auroka nodded. "Yes. In tunnels."

Rana gulped.

Brunois chuckled, saying, "That be scarin' ya then, Rana?"

She put on her brave face and said, "No! I just didn't think they would be underground is all. I was just thinking about how we'll see once we go in."

"Well, I suppose that ya might be able to be helpin' with that, eh? Seems like ya be the best suited fer havin' a bit o' fire to light the way."

That prospect was no comfort to Rana.

"What about the firefly?" she asked. "Do you think it might be able to light the way if you wind it enough?"

Brunois just remained silent, furrowing his brow and drawing his mouth. "Maybe," he finally conceded.

"She might be on to something with that, Brunois," Auroka said. "It does have that light on the end of it, and even in the light of Gassik's shop, it seemed quite bright."

"Yeah, Uncle Brunois, let's wind it up and see!"

Brunois frowned. "And what if it be flyin' off? Maybe we need it fer something once we get to the ruins."

"I don't think that will happen." The words had left Rana's mouth before Brunois had even stopped talking.

"It didn't seem to want to fly away when you wound it up in the shop," Auroka added. "It actually landed on your shoulder."

Brunois reached into his jacket and took out both the mechanical firefly and the winged key with which to wind it. He held both objects in front of him. The gleam of the fire flickered across the brass forms, giving them a warm radiance.

"Oh, just do it already!" Rana said.

Brunois looked over to Auroka, who also nodded her assent to the idea. He gave a single nod and inserted the key into the hole on the firefly's back. Instead of turning the key only a few turns, Brunois chose to wind it all the way. When he felt tension on the key from the firefly being fully wound, he took a deep breath and let it go.

Immediately, the little mechanical insect sprung to life, its wings beating the air. The light on its rear end began to shine, along with the strange little bug's eyes, all three glowing brightly. As it gained a bit of altitude, it began to fly in circles around the meager campsite.

The three watched on with the same sense of awe as when they first saw the thing. It would fly in long arcs and spirals, moving in between trees around the edge of the campsite. Its light would flicker on and off as it did, illuminating the surrounding woodlands with bright, staccato flashes.

After a full minute of circles, whoops, and whorls, the firefly returned to Brunois and hovered near him.

Brunois stared at it. It stared back. The little brass bug would move every few seconds but still continued to stare. Brunois swatted lightly at it, but the firefly easily evaded the half-hearted attempts.

"I think it likes you, Uncle Brunois!" Rana proclaimed. Her smile was so wide it looked as if her head might split entirely in two.

Auroka was quite amused as well. "It seems you've made a new friend, Brunois."

"I don't want me no new friends. And if this damn thing don't stop starin' at me, I might just smash the pesterin' thing."

Brunois looked straight at the firefly and croaked in a harsh tone, "Stop lookin' at me!"

It continued to stare. Rana and Auroka laughed.

The group spent another hour trying to communicate with the firefly, but to no avail. It just continued to hover near Brunois, moving erratically but always staying close. A few times, when a loud noise was heard, it would leave the Frog's side and fly to wherever the noise had originated. The little metal bug would linger there a moment, flickering its light and flying about before returning to Brunois's personal space.

"Yep, looks like you made a friend!" Rana said.

"Oh, this just be great," Brunois muttered. "Another pest what needs lookin' after."

10

The morning brought more annoyance for Brunois. The firefly lay on his chest, staring at him. Its eyes flickered.

"Whaddya want?" the Frog croaked out.

The firefly's eyes just flickered again. It beat its wings and lifted off of Brunois, only to come back down closer to his face.

Brunois sat up and swatted at the bug, muttering, "Bleedin' pest."

He blinked his eyes a few times, stood, stretched, and looked around. A rising sun shed light on the woods from a cloudless sky. Auroka was already up and packing her things. Rana snored lightly.

The firefly circled around to face Brunois again, hovering inches from his face.

Another swat at the bug. "Get away fro'me."

It did not listen.

Brunois stormed off.

It followed.

Rana stirred from her slumber. Her first act was to wrap her blanket around her as tightly as possible. Her second was to stare blankly at the campsite while her faculties awakened. That one took longer. When she had completed it, she looked around and saw her uncle trying to swat the firefly away.

"I was just about to wake you," Auroka said as she walked over to Rana. "We'll be heading out soon."

It didn't take Rana long to pack her things, and with Auroka's help, they were ready to move in half an hour.

Brunois spent most of that time trying to get the firefly to leave him alone. It was persistent.

They ate breakfast as they walked. The day was becoming quite nice, although the land was becoming increasingly hostile. Less vegetation grew as they got closer to the Wastes, and what did grow bore signs of taint and corruption.

They stopped to take their midday rest among a sickly grove of trees. The fruit on its branches looked like it grew already rotten.

As they ate, the firefly landed on Brunois's leg. It stared him in the eye.

"I think he wants something from you, Uncle Brunois," Rana said.

"I told ya not to be callin' me uncle."

The firefly took flight again and bumped into Brunois a few times on his chest then landed again on his leg. It resumed its stare.

"What is it, ya bleedin' pest?" Brunois stared back at it.

"Maybe he wants to be wound?" Auroka offered. "We need food and water, he needs to be wound."

"When did this thing become a 'he'?" Brunois asked.

Auroka and Rana shrugged in unison.

The firefly flew into the same spot on Brunois's chest again. Brunois reached to where it was nudging and got out the wind-up key.

He held it up, asking the bug, "This what ya be wantin' then?"

The firefly blinked once.

Brunois held out his hand and it landed there. He wound it.

When he was finished, the firefly sprung back to life and took up a position hovering near him.

"I think he's happy," Rana said.

Brunois snorted. "I don't think somethin' like that can be happy. It's just a mechanical bug. And what sort o' fool do I be fer talkin' to it?"

Rana watched the firefly hover by her uncle and said, "I think you should give him a name."

"Why would I want to be doin' that?"

"I agree," Auroka chimed in.

"The both of ya be crazy. I ain't namin' it."

"Let's call him Blinky," Rana declared.

Auroka smiled. "I like it. Very cute. Blinky."

"I ain't gonna call it Blinky," Brunois croaked.

Auroka shrugged.

"Well, what are you going to call him then?" Rana asked.

Brunois frowned and looked at the firefly as it hovered. It turned enough to look back at him.

"The pest," he finally said.

"The pest? That's not a very nice name..." Rana pouted.

"So?"

"Can't you name him something a little nicer?" Rana's voice took on the manipulative quality unique to teenage girls.

Brunois snorted. "Fine, iffn' it'll get ya to be shuttin' up. I'll call him the Peste."

"That's the same name."

"Nah, it be spelled different." Brunois laughed at his own joke.

Auroka laughed a little too.

Rana did not laugh. She pouted. "Hmph."

"We should get moving again if we want to make the outpost by sunset," Auroka said as she rose.

The two Frogs nodded and stood.

The four members of the party moved out.

11

"There it is," Auroka said.

"What?" asked Rana.

"The trader's outpost."

Rana gaped. "That?"

The group stood at the edge of a clearing, looking at a cluster of shanties. Strewn about the ground were all manner of rusted equipment and mechanisms of unknown purpose. A harsh, dry wind blew through. Stillness reigned.

"Looks like no one's here," Rana murmured.

Brunois and Auroka exchanged a look. *Careful.*

They stepped into the clearing and began navigating the debris field. There was a decrepit wagon, a bin of cogs and gears, several barrels, a piece of farming equipment. The Peste buzzed about Brunois as they went.

One contraption looked akin to the skeleton of a giant bird. A set of wings spanned the central framework of its body for ten feet on either side. The body itself had no walls and was filled with two benches behind a captain's chair and some sort of engine. At its back was a vertical tail.

"What do you suppose it is?" Rana wondered aloud. She ran her hands over it as she examined the engine.

"Looks to be some sort o' flyin' machine. Probably no works," Brunois said.

Auroka glanced at it. "I think it did at one point. I doubt anyone built it out here or transported it some other way."

Brunois shrugged. He continued his search for any sign of life.

The Peste turned to face the edge of the clearing, its light blinking. A figure crashed through the corrupted vegetation. It ran fast and low, a rifle in its hand, and dove behind one of the shanties.

Auroka and Brunois immediately ducked behind cover. Rana didn't duck until gunfire pierced the air.

A gruff voice rang out, "You won't get me so easy!"

The figure poked out from behind the corrugated metal of the shanty and returned fire.

Auroka leaned into Brunois. "That's Jahn. The owner of this place. He's former Royal Army."

Brunois nodded. His revolvers were already in his hands. He cocked them.

Rana looked to her uncle for some guidance. He didn't notice, so she pressed harder into the rock she had hidden behind.

"Got yerself a plan then?" Brunois asked Auroka.

"Cover me," she replied with a wink. She unslung her bow and stalked off toward the woods.

Brunois stood from behind his cover and began to shoot at an even pace. Since he didn't have targets, the goal was to force them to keep cover while Auroka flanked them. The Peste took off in the direction he was shooting.

Auroka moved through the sick forest, her hooves soundless as she went. A flicker caught her attention. *The Peste?* She moved toward it. Her quarry came into view, a group of Rodents. She took a deep breath and focused. A shimmering arrow crackled into existence as she drew her bow. She loosed it.

The Weasel was sent flying through the air from the force. He struck a tree and fell to the ground, smoke drifting off his body.

The second arrow was on its way before the rest of the Rodents knew what happened. This time it was a Ferret hurled through the air with a sizzling pop. Panic set in among them.

Auroka sighted another Ferret. The arrow flew. Her target was struck in the back and sent soaring. She watched the remaining three run back toward the Wastes.

"Auroka?" the gruff voice called out.

"Hello, Jahn," she called back. Bow still in hand, she walked back toward the cluster of shanties.

Brunois had appeared from behind his cover and was trading uneasy glances with the Mule named Jahn. Rana remained hidden.

"He's all right," Auroka said to both of them. "You can come out too if you want, Rana."

A smile appeared on Jahn's face as Auroka approached. "It's good to see you again," he told her.

"Good to see you too."

She didn't mean it. He looked awful. His gray hair was mottled. His woolen clothing was varying shades of brown, from varying degrees of dirt. Most of it was ripped and tattered.

"When I saw the flashes, I thought it had to be you." Jahn looked over the others. "Who are your friends?"

"Jahn, this is Brunois and Rana." Auroka looked at the two Frogs and the Peste, who was now hovering near them. "And the little one we call the Peste."

Jahn nodded at the trio. "Pleased to meet you sir, miss, and…bug." He looked over all four. "Not that I'm ungrateful, but might I ask what all of you are doing out here?"

"We're on an adventure!" Rana proclaimed.

Brunois rolled his eyes. Auroka laughed. The Peste blinked a single time.

"I see…" Jahn replied.

Auroka intervened. "We're on our way to a Svargan ruin in the Wastes."

"Iffn' I might be askin', who was they just now ya be runnin' from? And should we be thinkin' they may be comin' back?" Brunois gave Jahn an inquisitive look.

"Oh, they'll likely be back, but not for a few weeks or so. They make a run at me about once a month. They're just a pack of Rodent scavengers. Of course, this time they got it much worse than they usually do."

A grin flashed across Auroka's face. "We should probably do something about their bodies before they attract undue attention."

"Nonsense!" Jahn said. "You are all my guests, and rescuers it would seem, although I wasn't really in need of rescue. Nevertheless, you did chase them off and I am in your debt. I will tend to their bodies later, but for now, let us have a spot of tea?"

Rana leapt at the idea. "I'd love tea! What kind is it?"

"Well, little miss, it's a special blend I get from across the sea," Jahn replied. "Let's go inside and I'll put a pot on."

They all went to the largest of the shanties. It didn't look much better on the inside. The metal walls were rusted and pitted, with light pouring through several holes. A few pieces of worn, rickety furniture sat toward the center of the single room, trying not to break under the strain of time.

Jahn walked over to a woodstove and began to place some kindling and a few logs in it. "Now where are those matches…" he mumbled, fishing around through a number of disorderly shelves.

A smile plastered to her face, Rana walked up and pointed her hand at the open door of the stove. She narrowed her eyes, clenched her jaw, and shot a jet of fire in. The dry wood burst into flames.

Jahn gave the young Frog a look and nodded. "Why, thank you, miss."

Rana's smile grew even bigger. "You're welcome."

Jahn filled a teapot with some water from a barrel and set it on the stove. "Now then, that shouldn't take long."

"That flying machine out there," Rana asked, "does it work?"

Jahn shook his head. "Not really. It does function, but the problem is that enough fuel to heat the boiler to fly far makes it too heavy to fly."

Rana nodded. "How did it get out here then?"

"The folks who built it had some kind of relic they put in the boiler. They brought the whole thing out here when this place was still a military outpost and did some experiments. After a few weeks, they got called back to work on something else and just left it there." Jahn sighed. "I tried my darndest to get it working again, but just couldn't figure how to heat the boiler and still be light enough to fly. Maybe with your talent there you can heat it?"

Rana grinned. "I would love to!"

Brunois snorted. "Yer welcome to stay 'ere and fiddle 'round with it iffn' ya want, Rana, but I mean to keep movin' on to th'ruins what we set out fer to begin with."

Rana's face sank.

"Don't worry, Rana," Auroka offered. "If we find anything out at the ruins, there will probably be some time for you to come here and work on it."

"That would be nice…" Rana sighed.

Auroka turned to Jahn and asked, "Might we spend the night here? We'll leave first thing in the morning, and if you have them, we would like to buy some supplies."

Jahn chuckled. "Of course you can sleep here tonight. And I do have provisions that you can have."

"We will, of course, pay for them, Jahn." Auroka looked the Mule in the eye.

He chuckled again. "As you wish then."

A shrill whistle blew out of the teapot.

Jahn walked over and took it off the stove. "But for now, let us have our tea."

CHAPTER

12

The Dunham Constabulary Headquarters was in disarray. The holding cells were full of foul-mouthed thugs. There was a line of citizens waiting to lodge complaints. The magistrate's office had a minimum two-day wait to be seen. It was a day like any other.

Inspector Wourinos fought his way through the great clawing masses and ducked into his own office. It had taken him many years to earn it. It didn't have a nice view, and it wasn't lavishly decorated, but it was his. After shutting the door, he poured himself a drink out of a cut glass decanter on the sideboard. The scotch warmed his body.

This past week had set his nerves on edge. Despite being the sort that lived his life by intuition, he preferred to have reliable information with which to make decisions. He had only coincidences. He didn't like coincidences.

First, a Svargan artifact is stolen from the Museum of Antiquities. A pack of thugs led by Rache is suspected. Then, one of the deputy constables claims to have seen Brunois Bonne'Chance fleeing the scene of a gunfight. Left for dead there was a Dog, known to be one of Rache's. A few days later, Rache and the remainder of his pack assaulted a known fence for stolen merchandise, then took off.

It annoyed Wourinos that he had only learned of the event at Gassik's Pawnbrokerage today. *Rache could be anywhere now. Brunois too. But what does Gassik have to do with all of this?*

He meant to find out.

There was a knock at the door.

"Enter," Wourinos called out.

The door opened, and Gassik was led in by a deputy constable, who deposited him in the chair across from Wourinos's desk and then left.

"Good evening, sir. My name is Inspector Wourinos. I'd like to ask you a few questions."

"What am I doing here?" Gassik hissed at the inspector.

"Answering my questions. Let's go back to the assault. Rache and four other Dogs entered your store and accosted you about a week ago, yes?"

Gassik wrinkled his snout. "Yep."

"Why?"

"They wanted to rob me."

"And yet they took very little. Why is that?"

"I stalled them as best I could. Guess they figured that after so much time had gone by, they should just leave."

"Were they asking you about a specific item?"

"No."

Wourinos stared at Gassik.

"Do you know a Frog named Brunois Bonne'Chance?" Wourinos asked.

"No."

Wourinos paused to stare at Gassik before saying, "Sir, if you continue to lie to me, I will see to it that your business is shut down. You are a known fence of stolen goods, and I would happily station a constable at your store twenty-four hours a day. Furthermore, I will see to it that all your financial records are audited by the Royal Tax Secretary, and when they uncover fraud within your ledgers, I will see to it that you are sent to prison for an exceedingly long time."

Gassik shifted in the chair.

Wourinos had selected that chair personally. The seat was flat and hard, and the back tilted slightly forward. Sitting on it was quite an uncomfortable experience.

"So I ask you again, sir, what was Rache after within your shop?"

Gassik let out a sigh. "An egg."

"An egg?"

"Well, a Svargan artifact that rather looked like an egg."

"The one that was stolen from the Museum of Antiquities?"

Gassik shrugged. "I don't know. Could have been, but I didn't recognize it."

Wourinos nodded. "And did you have it at the time?"

Gassik nodded.

"And how did you come into possession of it?"

"It was given to me."

"By who?"

"Brunois Bonne'Chance."

"He gave it to you?"

"In exchange for a service."

"And this service?"

"I connected him with someone who could act as a guide for somewhere he wanted to go."

"And where was that?"

"A suspected place for a Svargan ruin, out in the Wastes."

"And who was this guide?"

"A Horse named Auroka."

Wourinos blinked. *Perfect.*

"The Horse's last name?"

"She said Firemane."

"You don't believe her?"

"I don't care one way or the other."

"When did this event happen?"

Gassik thought for a minute, counting on his fingers. "Nine days ago."

"And the incident with Rache was seven days ago?"

Gassik nodded.

"Do you know where they were headed?"

"Not exactly. Just east toward the Wastes."

"Did Rache learn all of this from you too?"

Gassik tensed up but then nodded. "Aye."

Wourinos stared at Gassik, appraising him.

"Anything else helpful you want to add?" Wourinos asked.

Gassik shook his head. "Nope. That's all of it. Am I free to go?"

Wourinos nodded. "You may leave, but I may be by before too long with more questions."

Gassik stood and left. He didn't say good-bye. He didn't close the door behind him.

Wourinos leaned back and put his paws behind his head. He stayed in that position for a while, breaking from it only to sip his scotch.

He ran through the chain of events again. *I'm still missing something.*

13

The sunrise was red when Auroka, Rana, Brunois, and the Peste set out from Jahn's outpost. Jahn had supplied them enough for a few days and insisted that they also stop on their way back for more. The Mule had only accepted payment under great pressure from Auroka.

Brunois wondered what was in their past but decided he didn't care.

The Peste had already begun its prodding of Brunois to wind it. Brunois swatted at it, croaking, "Get away fro'me. I'll wind ya when I'm good 'n' ready."

Rana trailed behind the others. Her belly was fuller than it had been in days, and she hadn't slept so well since first leaving Underbrook. Still, the rigors of the trail were hard on her, and their accumulated effect slowed her.

"I said get away fro'me!" Brunois croaked again.

The Peste was weaving an intricate pattern amongst the Frog's flailing hands.

"Oh, quit being so foolish and just wind him!" Rana croaked at her uncle.

Brunois blinked and turned to her, raising an eyebrow.

Rana was just as shocked as he at the outburst, but she stood her ground and held her gaze.

"Fine, iffn' it'll get th'both of ya to be settlin' down," Brunois conceded.

He held the palm of his hand up and produced the key. The Peste landed and was wound.

Auroka laughed a little at the whole incident but urged them on. "We'll need to keep the pace up if we want to make it there with some daylight left."

The landscape had become treacherous. Jagged rocks and dusty crags were everywhere. The vegetation had degraded to little more than brushy weeds, although it was quite voluminous in places. There were occasional deformed trees, their trunks twisted in anguish.

Around midday, they took a rest by a stagnant pool. Their rations were fresh, and Rana devoured two pieces of cornbread and a handful of dried apricot. She washed the food down with some water from a canteen Jahn had given her and then walked down to the edge of the putrid water. The Peste joined her.

Rana looked up at the hovering firefly. "Yeah, he doesn't like me much either."

A single blink.

She began to conjure little fireballs in her hands and toss them into the water, listening to the hiss of the steam when they hit the surface. *Why did he even let me come along if this is how he's going to treat me?*

The water stirred. First bubbles, then ripples, then a full out churning. A black tentacle shot out at Rana. She croaked and rolled to the side, barely evading it.

"Help!" she called out.

The Peste began blinking furiously.

A grotesque mass of teeth and tentacles surfaced. It gnashed at the air and issued wet, crunching sounds. Black tentacles of varying sizes undulated around the chomping maw. Two of them grabbed at Rana.

She was too horrified to scream again. She was too horrified to do anything.

The tentacles wrapped around her. They felt rubbery against her skin. Her mind had shut down from the shock of it all and her emotions overwhelmed her. Fear. Unrestrained, all-consuming fear. Everything around her began to fade.

Brunois heard the first scream for help and stood to scan the area. She was not in plain sight, but something was moving down in the water, so he took off that way.

Auroka followed him. Neither was prepared for what they saw.

Protruding from the putrid pool was an amorphous writhing. Its oily black form was difficult to distinguish from the water. Tentacles wriggled out from it in all directions. Two of them clutched a speck of red.

Brunois drew his sword and hopped from the ledge he was perched on. He swung it overhead in a smooth motion; the slice severed one of the tentacles encircling Rana. A spray of noxious fluid exploded out from the now separate ends.

He spun around and hacked at the other ghastly appendage gripping his niece. Another eruption of sickening liquid streamed out, but the sword did not go all the way through.

The tentacle convulsed and dropped Rana. The impact of her body on the ground was enough to jar her from the catatonic state she had fallen into. She blinked and wheezed as she sat up. The world came back into focus, and she saw her uncle, hopping and hacking at hideous snakes.

Brunois tried to retreat from the water. He was not successful. The thing in the pool was determined to have a prize and continued to grab and strike at the Frog. Brunois was determined to not be that prize. He stabbed and slashed at the tentacles as they tried to grasp him, hopping and leaping around to avoid their clutch.

Auroka stood on a rock, bow drawn, a blazing arrow readied, searching for a clear shot.

Amidst the tangle of blackness the Peste buzzed and weaved. Its light flickered, rapid and bright, as it dodged in between the plump appendages. Avoidance came easily to it.

Brunois hopped over a tentacle that swept at his feet. He landed and thrust his sword into another. More of the thing's fluids spilled out as he withdrew his weapon. He rolled out of the way as another tried to wrap itself around his torso.

A bright flash sent a wash of light over the area, accompanied by a hissing sizzle. Fingers of energy danced across the intermingled surfaces of water and creature. Auroka's arrow had found its mark. The tentacles withdrew, coiling around the central maw. The thing submerged back to the depths that had spawned it.

Everyone looked at each other. They breathed a collective sigh.

"Are you all right?" Auroka asked Rana.

The little red Frog nodded. "I think so…"

Brunois poked at a severed piece of the creature with his sword. "What manner o' beast be that?"

"I'm not sure, but I'm glad it's gone. Let's get away from here," Auroka answered.

Both Frogs nodded. The Peste blinked once.

Auroka helped Rana up to her feet, giving the young Frog her arm for support.

Brunois joined them. He glanced at Rana for a moment.

"I'm all right," Rana offered.

Brunois nodded. "Good."

14

The party's trek took on a different tone after the incident at the pool. They scanned their surroundings with every step, suspicious of every scorched rock and twisted plant. Even the Peste managed to communicate anxiety.

Tension turned to exhaustion. Rana began to slow down. Even Brunois had trouble maintaining the pace. The land revolted at their presence, spitting forth hissing fissures, streams of sludge, and plantlike abominations. Each step was harder than the last, and the three walking members of the group found themselves having to force their legs to keep moving.

The afternoon was late when Auroka held up a fist. They all came to a halt.

"We are here," she said.

Brunois and Rana looked around. They stood among a few small hills, littered with piles of rocks. Red-orange dust strafed across their faces, carried on a hot wind.

"I don't be seein' nothin'," Brunois croaked.

"Me neither," said Rana.

The Peste blinked a single time. It was having a hard time with the wind gusts, frequently being blown away and having to circle back to Brunois.

Auroka hopped off of a ledge and waved everyone else over. When they arrived, she was standing in front of a door cut into the side of a hill. It had a symbol of a firefly carved in it. The Peste buzzed and flickered.

Brunois looked at Auroka. "So then, how we be gettin' in?"

Auroka looked back. "Don't you have a key?"

"Not fer that, just fer the Peste."

Rana walked up to the doors and began to examine them. "There's lots of little, odd-shaped holes here. What do you suppose they're for?" She placed her fingers in one, feeling the smooth edges of it.

Brunois approached the doors and laid his hand on the central firefly symbol. In its back was a hole. He stared into it but only saw blackness. He felt a nudge on his shoulder and looked up to see the Peste staring at him.

He backed away a little and watched the tiny brass firefly land on the edge of the opening and then crawl in. Brief flickers of light flashed inside the hole, then stopped.

They all waited and stared at the doorway.

A loud knock broke their reverie. The sound was followed by a whirring noise, and the doors slid back from where they met, disappearing into the side of the rocky hill. A great darkness opened before them. It was lit by staccato flashes of light from the Peste, which hovered in the tunnel.

"You opened the door!" Rana exclaimed.

Brunois and Auroka shared a look.

"In we go then?" Brunois asked.

Auroka nodded as she picked up a large rock and placed it on the threshold of the doorway. "Just in case the door tries to close."

They joined the Peste deeper into the entryway. Metallic surfaces reflected the firefly's intermittent flashes. The walls themselves were made of dark brown stone blocks, but running along them were tubes of steel, brass, and copper, which fed into various boxes and contraptions.

"Rana, you think ya can be conjurin' us a flame what we can use to light our way then?" Brunois asked.

Rana nodded and took a deep breath, but before she could do anything, the Peste landed on a spot near them and began to flicker excitedly.

It sat on the circular handle to a valve. A metal tube ran up from it, along the wall, and then down the tunnel along the ceiling. Glass lamps hung from it at regular intervals.

Rana studied the valve. "I think this may turn those lamps on."

"Ya be willin' to risk yer life on that?" Brunois asked.

"No…I suppose not," she answered.

"Then best to be leavin' it be. No tellin' what manner o' trap be down here. And fer that matter, even if it was no meant to be a trap, it might just be broken and kill us all the same. Best not be touchin' anything at all."

Auroka shrugged. "I agree with Rana. I think we should try it. They look like gas lights, and that is probably the tube that feeds them the gas."

Brunois began to speak, but before he could get a word out, Rana had already begun to turn the valve. A slight hiss could be heard, but no light came. He breathed a sigh of relief and said, "Well, at least ya didn't get us all killed. Now turn it off."

Rana frowned but then began to stare at the first in the row of lamps. Her eyes narrowed, and she raised her hands. A tiny flame sprung to life in the lamp. Then the next. She relaxed as the tunnel was lit by degrees going downward. The self-satisfied smirk she threw at her uncle felt good.

The descent down the sloping tunnel was slow going. Not that there were any obstacles to navigate, but the group took caution with each step and carefully studied their environment as they went. It was a single tube with no branches or other doorways the group could discern. Symbols painted in white marked the walls and other apparatuses.

"Is this the language of the Svargans?" Rana asked.

Auroka nodded, her coppery ringlets shimmering slightly in the warm light of the gas lamps. "It is. I recognize some of it."

Rana's face lit up. "Can you read any of it?"

Auroka shook her head. "No, I cannot."

Rana pouted.

"Don't seem like there be anythin' here," Brunois croaked.

"Have some patience, Brunois," Auroka said. "This tunnel is clearly just a means of access to something. I would think that anything placed this deep within the ground is something worth protecting. My guess would be this was a Svargan military outpost of some type."

Brunois glanced over at the Horse. "What makes ya be sayin' that?"

"Look at the walls and the floor," Auroka answered. "They are well made, but just the bare essentials, so it probably wasn't a living space. And it's probably not a mine, or we would see something by which they got their material out. This is all just speculation on my part, but I think you would agree it has the feel of being military."

"Maybe we find some weapons then," Brunois mused. "The army be payin' a fine price fer Svargan arms. Maybe even find somethin' I just keep fer m'self too. Never know when ya be needin' a good weapon."

They turned a corner in the tunnel and came to a crossway. Only the path they had come from was illuminated. The darkness of the other three stretched infinitely.

"Well then, which way we be wantin' to try then?" Brunois asked turning to face the others. He noticed the Peste was not with them.

"Where did that fool bug get to?" he asked.

The Peste shot out of the tunnel they had walked down, blinking furiously. None of them had even noticed it had lingered back. It began buzzing around them in a frantic flicker. They all staggered back a little to avoid it.

"What is it, you bleedin' bug?" Brunois croaked as he swatted at it.

A volley of bullets struck the ground where they had been standing.

CHAPTER

15

Rache surveyed the doorway. How thoughtful of them to leave it propped open for me. The door was made from two thick plates of steel. A symbol of a firefly was divided in half by the opening in the middle. Beyond it was an illuminated tunnel, diving into the earth.

The party had been easy to track. The Horse was quite good, leaving only an occasional sign of her passing, and the larger of the two Frogs wasn't too bad either. But the smaller Frog, whoever they were, was easily followed. Rache judged he had even made better time than his quarry since he didn't have any such dead weight to drag along, and their scent had grown stronger as the pack pursued them.

It had taken them only a week to reach the outpost. Rache had to laugh a little at the way that grizzled old Mule had gotten the drop on Duggar, who had been sent to scout. The gray Mutt had quietly snaked his way up through the trash field that surrounded the few makeshift buildings in the center. He peeked over a box of scraps to discover two barrels of a scattergun staring at him.

Rache hadn't wanted to sacrifice his right hand Dog, so the group continued to follow the eastward trail their prey had left.

The pack had begun to mutter when they came upon a piece of black, rubbery flesh rotting in the sun. Its serpentine form was thick and bulbous and clearly part of something much larger.

"Stay away from th'water," Rache had barked at them.

Now they stood at the gateway to whatever subterranean ruin lay below.

"I don't like this, boss. I think—" Grimley was cut off by Rache's paw knocking him to the ground.

"If I needed ya to do any thinkin' fer me, I'd have died long ago," Rache instructed the lesser Dog.

The pack was muttering again.

Rache turned to face them, letting the weight of alpha male be felt. "Duggar, Grimley. Yer in first."

"How come I gotta go first?" Grimley whined.

"Cause if ya die, I miss ya th'least," Rache told him. "Now get in there and keep yer voices down. No tellin' how close the Frogs and the Horse be."

Grimley hesitated but did as commanded. He and Duggar slid through the opening in the door and looked around. The tunnel inside was well lit by a row of lamps hung from the ceiling. Tubes, pipes, boxes, and other contraptions lined the walls. None of it looked particularly dangerous.

Duggar nodded to Grimley, who in turn poked his head out of the opening and gave the all clear sign.

The rest of the pack entered and began to walk quietly down the tunnel. Grimley was on point, followed by Duggar and Rache, with Stick and Spade at the rear. Weapons were drawn, loaded, and cocked. Ears forward, eyes alert, noses open. The steps of their paws were light as they stalked downward. They would have their prey.

And then, whatever is here will be ours. Rache relished this thought almost as much as the prospect of running that fool Frog, Brunois, through with his sword.

A blinking light appeared from beyond a curve in the tunnel. Grimley held up a paw and the pack came to a stop. They all stared at the light, trying to discern what it was. Guns came up as stances turned to crouches.

The flickering light disappeared back around the bend.

The pack crept forward, wary of what they were going to find.

Voices drifted up to them. Their owners came into view, standing at a landing with other tunnels leading away from it.

The Dogs all looked to Rache. He nodded. *Open fire.*

CHAPTER

16

Another spurt of gunfire rattled off the floor. Brunois, Auroka, and Rana crouched behind some metal boxes in a darkened tunnel. They were pinned down with nowhere to go except further into the darkness.

The Peste hovered near them, intermittently blinking.

Brunois swatted at it, hissing in a low voice, "Stop yer bleedin' blinkin', ya foul thing!"

He was thankful it had saved their lives by alerting them to the first barrage of bullets. He hoped it would now not get them all killed.

The blinks continued. Each flash illuminated the space around them briefly, reflecting off the metal surfaces and casting short-lived shadows. They all knew it would only be a matter of time before the attackers realized their position.

Brunois peeked out from behind their cover. He didn't see anyone. While it was possible that they could be attacking from one of the other darkened tunnels, he doubted it very much. It seemed more likely they had followed the same downward slope that he had walked, which meant they couldn't see his group yet either.

Auroka stared at him, asking the silent question, "What did you see?"

Brunois leaned in and whispered, "Can't see any of 'em right now, so if we're gonna move, now be the best time fer it. Let's start us crawlin' further down this tunnel. Iffn' we can find a good position what to defend from, maybe we can take a stand long 'nough what we can see how many of 'em there be."

Auroka nodded.

Rana gulped then nodded. Her eyes widened beyond any normal constraints, and she set herself firmly on all fours.

They began to crawl into the inky blackness of the unknown. The ground was surprisingly warm to their hands, but rather than bringing comfort, it brought trepidation. It felt unnatural.

Still flashing, the Peste followed them. As much as Brunois dreaded that light giving their position away, the occasional flicker served to give them at least some bearing.

Auroka stayed alongside Rana. The little Frog was shaking, the vibrations being felt by Auroka through the floor. As travel permitted, she would place a reassuring hand on Rana's back. It would still the tremors, even if just for a moment.

A large battery of metal contraptions provided them a temporary refuge. They ducked behind it, the Peste staying close by, still blinking. Their crawl down the tunnel had been about ten minutes long. Brunois wondered how much distance they had put between them and their hunters.

"This be a good spot I think. Lots o' cover, and that doorway we passed through back there make a good choke point so they can no just rush in at us. Hopefully we get some sort o' chance to be thinnin' their numbers out a bit." Brunois's voice was low.

A flash from the Peste illuminated the room. The barrier they hid behind looked to be some type of desk, with many switches, dials, and other instruments mounted on it. Several of these circled the room and in the center was another smaller version of it. Hatches and doorways lined the walls and even the floor. Many were rusted and corroded.

"I think we could hold a few here, if we had to, but there's no telling just how many. I'm going to scout a retreat plan should we need to use it." Auroka nodded to the others and moved back out into the room, crouching low.

Brunois nodded and turned to Rana, asking, "Ya think iffn' ya had to you could toss a fireball?"

Rana remained silent but nodded. The stare on her face was focused on something Brunois could not see, and her eyes did not move as she nodded her head.

Guns drawn, hammers cocked, Brunois waited. It was only a matter of time, but at least he got to dictate the terms of the fight this time. He was confident that they could fell one or two before any more could reach their position. Depending on how many they had, that could make all the difference.

Another flicker.

Brunois swatted at the bug again, doing his best to yell at it without raising his voice so much that others heard. "Iffn' yer gonna be about, go wait by th'doorway and signal when the others come, eh? Ya might as well be doin' somethin' what be a help to us, 'stead of just riskin' us gettin' shot."

The Peste gave a single blink and then flew off to where the tunnel bottlenecked at a doorway of sorts.

"Bleedin' thing actually went and stood guard…" Brunois wondered aloud, more to himself than anyone else.

"There are a lot of doors," Auroka said as she slipped back among the other two. "Most of them lead to single rooms, but there is one, on the rear wall, that appears to lead to another series of tunnels. If we have to retreat, that's the place."

Another flicker.

"Sounds good then, let's hope we don't be needin' to," Brunois replied. His gaze was locked upon the doorway where the Peste had stationed itself.

Auroka unslung her bow and gripped the string but did not draw it back. A slight scuffling noise reached her ears. She tensed up but then forced herself to relax with a deep breath.

They stared into the darkness, searching for some distinction in the black on black wash that enveloped them. The ancient tunnels remained silent, still, stoic. Secrets had been locked within them for ages; it was not in their nature to reveal anything.

Another flicker.

A silhouette was given substance as the light from the Peste wrapped around it. It stood on the far side of the threshold.

Flicker.

The form appeared on the other side of the threshold, legs in full stride, rifle rising.

Flicker.

Two paces in, rifle leveled.

Gunshots rang out, their echo endless off the walls.

Flicker.

The form lay on its back, rifle several feet away. Its chest did not move, nor any other part of it.

Brunois ducked back behind the cover of the odd metal desk. Smoke drifted out of the barrels of his revolvers. They were still cocked. The room was now in constant flux between light and dark as the Peste continued to flicker.

Auroka risked a peek. More forms, Canine-looking forms, appeared on the far side of the threshold. She began to draw her bow, but the clang of a bullet striking metal drove her back into hiding.

"Keep yer firin' even, boys, and advance steady, we got 'em pinned," a voice called out.

Brunois croaked a single word. "Rache."

The Peste rejoined them, fleeing the advance of the pack of Dogs. Bullets chased it but could not find the little brass firefly as it zigged and zagged its way through the stale air of the subterranean space.

"Time to be goin' then. Rana, can ya be throwin' a big fireball at 'em?" Brunois stared at his niece.

She was trembling, but she managed a "yes" and took a deep breath. Holding her hands in front of her, she glared and began to inhale and exhale in a forceful fashion. A searing ball of flame ignited in the space between her palms. It grew rapidly. She tossed it over the metal wall of their hiding place.

Yips, yowls, and yotes pierced through the roar of the fire. An orange glow warmed the air; the heat was felt even on the other side of the metal desk where Rana crouched.

"Now!" Brunois croaked.

The three of them, trailed closely by the Peste, took off in a low run toward the rear door of the chamber. The metal grates of the floor clanged as the party clamored over them, seeking safety through the steel gateway.

Auroka reached the door first, opening it fully from the propped position she had left it. Brunois dove in as soon as there was space enough to do so, rolling out of the way to allow the others to enter. The Peste buzzed past, light blazing.

A scream. It was Rana's.

Auroka turned her head in enough time to see the little red Frog disappear through an open grate in the floor.

"Rana!" she called out.

For reply, all she got was more rifle shots pinging the steel plate and frame of the doorway she crouched within. Having no choice, she ducked inside and slammed it shut, spinning a wheel blindly in the dark to lock it.

The Peste flickered to life, holding a steady glow to illuminate the space they now crouched within.

Brunois looked up at Auroka. "Rana?" he asked.

A sigh came from the Horse. "She fell through one of the open spots in the grated floor. I do not know where it leads, or how far down it goes."

Brunois nodded. The light from the Peste rippled across his eyes, they were deeper than before.

"Nothin' we can be doin' fer her right now. Nothin' we can be doin' here 'xcept dyin'. We need to be movin' b'fore they get through th'door." His voice was hollow.

They set off into the darkness, with the Peste to light the way.

CHAPTER

17

It was warm and dark. The disparate pairing caused Rana to be even more fearful.

Terror threatened to overwhelm her. She tried to fight it back. She was unsuccessful. The raw dread gripped her little heart and strangled all the willpower out of it.

No. I won't let this happen. I won't just lay here and die. Get up, Rana. Get up.

She struggled to her feet. The fall down had not been kind to her already harried body. The rigors of the trek leading to this place had left her on the border of total exhaustion. Tumbling down that metal shaft and being spit out onto a hard stone floor had felt like being run through the milling stones back home.

Her body revolted, giving out at the knees and sending her down onto all fours. Breathing required full conscious effort, and even then, only came with great pain and struggle. The world swirled around her in all its eldritch blackness. It was suffocating. It was dizzying. She closed her eyes and focused.

Inhale.

Exhale.

Inhale.

Exhale.

Breath by breath, the tremors that wracked her huddled form abated. The fantastic vortex of darkness slowed its sickening gyrations. Her faculties returned to her. She could feel the stone under her palms, mildly warm to the touch. She could smell the stale air that hung languidly within this subterranean place; something sweet and bitter threaded through it.

She made another attempt to rise to her feet. She managed, and stood totally still in total darkness. Her eyes opened, but there was still no light—just the same black expanse of emptiness.

After several more minutes of simply being alive, she raised her right hand and conjured a small flame. The cavernous space around her became illuminated with a warm, orange glow. The walls here were not the mortared blocks of the other tunnels but simply carved out spaces in the stone. Metal tubes and wires still ran across them, but rather than running in straight lines, they formed a web without any clear distinction of beginning or ending.

Rana turned in a complete circle, studying everything. The space was massive, and she could make out no clear sign of a path or doorway, save the opening to the chute she had plunged through. It was several feet up the wall, too far for her to climb back up into.

One at a time, Rana began to place her feet in front of each other and explore her surroundings. The light from the flame she kept was sufficient, and she found she could control its size without too much exertion. The fire was becoming second nature to her.

Now that she was out in the world, she had found freedom to use her gift. Not that her father had ever discouraged it outright, but after the incident at the mill, he had been so upset that she had stuffed the ability down as something bad—a defect. He had not meant to cause that feeling in his daughter, but she could only see disappointment. She could only see disgust.

———•◆•———

It had been a severe drought that summer. Crops everywhere were failing. The farmers banded together to do the best they could to irrigate their fields, but it didn't help much. To make matters worse, with all the new channels for the river to feed, its level had gone down even more. The waterwheel on the mill house stopped receiving enough pressure.

Arcator had been trying to narrow up the banks in the hope that bottlenecking the flow of the water would help to generate more pressure to turn the wheel. Rana, not even ten at the time, was helping her daddy however she could. Shovel in hand, she strained to move the dirt. She closed her eyes and clenched her jaw, struggling against a rock she didn't know her shovel was beneath. Her chest tightened as she expelled the last of her breath. Nothing.

She threw the shovel and stamped her feet, screaming out her frustrations. They leapt from her hands in the form of great, blazing torrents of fire. The wooden waterwheel ignited. The flame spread across it rapidly and began to encircle the wooden axle.

Arcator ran over with his shovel and began using it to turn the waterwheel. He had diverted the river for the sake of being able to work on the wheel, but there was still a pool of water where it sat—just enough to cover the bottom two or so feet. With each thud of the metal spade against the burning wood, the wheel turned a little more, quenching another section of flame. A full turn was enough to contain the fire, and a few buckets' worth later, it was completely out.

The mill house had been saved. The waterwheel was destroyed.

———— ◆•◆ ————

I didn't mean to do it. The memory swept Rana up in its tide, ushering her back to the edge of despair.

She resisted its pull. The flame in her hand doubled in size, and she had to toss it away to avoid being burned.

It danced across the ground in a vibrant wave, revealing a place where the stone floor turned to metal. Rana conjured another in her hand and went to investigate.

There was no seam where the metal ended; it just continued to thin as it spread over the stone, similar to how ice on a frozen pond encroaches onto dry land. The walls were covered in the same manner, and the myriad of other metallic apparatuses on them was now so prolific as to obscure her view of what lay beneath.

She looked forward again in the direction she had been walking and strained to see as far as she could. There were glints of more metal off in the distance.

She took a risk and lobbed her fireball, scanning the illuminated areas as it went past them. It struck the floor and gave a final flash of light, revealing hundreds of structures.

They were most definitely made of metal, but did not look as if they had been built. They looked as if they had *grown* out of the floor, walls, and ceiling. A vast field of metallic eggs and cocoons.

18

Brunois and Auroka journeyed deeper into the bowels of the tunnels, walking within an orb of light created by the Peste. The glow of its light gave a soft quality to the otherwise hard lines and bulky shapes of the block and metal. Nerves were on edge for both of them as they went; each stray noise or sudden change of shadow caused them to halt. To wait.

"Ya think they be able to get through that door?" Brunois asked.

Auroka didn't look at Brunois but answered, "It's hard to say, but I doubt it. I know it didn't have a way to unlock it from their side, so they will have to break it down somehow."

The light from the Peste flickered.

Brunois looked up at the little mechanical bug. It was still buzzing along, dutifully filling the role of "torch."

The light on its rear flickered again and dimmed a little.

Brunois took the key out of his jacket pocket and held up his palm for the Peste. It made a few circles first but then landed. He wound it back up, and it returned to its "torch" duties with renewed brilliance.

Brunois sighed. "Ya think Rana survived th'fall?"

Auroka sighed back. "I honestly do not know. It's possible. I think that grate led to some kind of ventilation tube. If she could manage to slow her fall through it, maybe it let her out somewhere safe. Somewhere we can find her."

"Guess we start lookin' then."

They came to a landing, with more tunnels sloping down and away from it. The Peste flew into the center of the space and shone light upon everything. There were piles of crates and boxes. Some of them were wooden.

"Ya be seein' that?" Brunois asked Auroka, nodding to one of the crates.

"What about it?" she returned.

"It be wooden. And it no appears to be the sort o' wood what's been cured to last fer hundreds o' years. Just some ordinary crate," Brunois remarked as he bent over to examine its contents.

The Peste joined him, posting itself over top of the crate to illuminate the contents.

"So we aren't the first to be in this place since the Svargans," she walked over to join him. "Where did you say you got that key from again? The one you use to wind the Peste?"

Brunois shot her a wry look out of the corner of his eye. "It was m'Grandpop's. I no be sure how he came to be in possession of it. I do know he was a soldier though. Served durin' the Reformatory War."

"Is it possible he was here during that time? This place would have been within the area of conflict."

"I thinkin' it not only be possible, I be thinkin' it likely. I was always thinkin' grandpop was a strange sort, tellin' tales from the war that none o' us ever believed were true. Least not after we was older than six. But he'd keep tellin' 'em. Stories 'bout giant mechanical monsters what shook th'ground with they feet, and horrible machines what took the livin' and burned 'em as fuel."

"Fantastic stories indeed."

"I'm beginnin' to think they weren't as make-believe as I thought they were." Brunois looked up from the box. "Ain't nothin' useful in 'ere. Best we keep movin' I think. Ya reckon which direction we want to be headin' iffn' we means to find Rana?"

All three tunnels looked equally forbidding; empty mouths waiting to swallow whatever, or whoever, might come their way. The stillness was dizzying. Nothing stirred, nothing moved. This far below the surface, there had been no fresh air for years.

Auroka shook her head and said, "I do not know. This place is so disorienting." Her words were full of apprehension.

"Well, I means to be findin' her 'fore that pack o' Dogs does, so let's get ourselves movin' then." He walked over toward the left-most tunnel.

"You really care about her, don't you?" Auroka asked.

Brunois balked. "What? No. Why ya be thinkin' that?"

"You certainly seem very concerned about her now."

The Frog's eyes narrowed, and he leveled his gaze at the Horse. "She be family, nothin' more."

Auroka scoffed. "You might be a good liar most of the time, but I can see through it this time. You really care for her."

Brunois glared. Hard. "I don't be needin' no one. I can get on fine by m'self. I do better by m'self, in fact."

"Nonsense. No one is meant to be alone."

"I am. 'Sides, what makes ya think I would be wantin' to be close with her? She's just a kid. Still be in her teen years." His voice was becoming heated.

"Be that as it may, you like having her around."

The Peste drifted over to Brunois and landed on his shoulder.

He looked over at it, and it back at him.

"Bah! Don't ya start in now with me too," he croaked at it.

The Peste's glassy eyes stared back at Brunois. Their emptiness was piercing. The little firefly gave a single blink.

"Ah, fine then. I do be carin' fer the little pain in m'neck. Ya happy?"

The Peste blinked once.

Auroka was happy too. She smiled, saying, "I told you I knew you were lying."

"Fine, ya were right, I care about her. Let's just get to findin' her then, eh?" He stalked off toward the tunnel on the left.

The Peste flew in front of him and blinked twice.

"What more ya want fro'me? I wound ya. I gave in to yer stupid eyes starin' at me. Now get out of m'way," he croaked angrily as he swatted at it.

The Peste easily evaded his swings and then blinked twice.

"I think it's telling us not to go this way," Auroka offered.

"It be a fool bug, what make ya think it know th'way to go?" he countered, still swatting at it as he tried to move into the tunnel.

"How daft are you? It comes from this place. It opened the top side door. It saved our lives when we were attacked back there. I'm more inclined to trust its judgment than yours at this point." Her voice was getting fiery as she spoke.

"Listen to yerself! Ya sayin' we should be takin' orders from a bleedin' piece o' machinery? It be a bug, and a mechanical one at that. Thing wouldn't even do nothing 'cept I be windin' it regular." Another swing and a miss as the Peste weaved under his arm.

It flew over to the middle tunnel and blinked a single time.

Brunois glared at Auroka.

Auroka beamed. "See?"

"I be loathin' the both of ya," he croaked out so gruffly that Auroka was certain rocks had come out of his mouth.

The middle tunnel was well lit by the Peste when Brunois began to walk down it. He stared hard at Auroka. He stared hard at the Peste.

The Peste blinked once as Auroka went by.

"I know," she said to the little firefly with a strained laugh. "I know."

CHAPTER

19

Rache cursed bitterly at the door. It wouldn't budge. He kicked it with his heel, not trying to do any real damage but just letting his anger out.

The surviving Dogs in his pack shifted around the room, examining the floor and other doorways. They had lit some simple torches, and the room was illuminated enough for a good inspection. All four of them did their best not to look at Grimley's corpse, which lay where it fell, now stripped of its gear.

The hole in the floor grating, which Rana had plummeted into, was being probed by Duggar. The brown Mutt's head was halfway into the empty space beneath the floor, his torch being held at a distance so as not to pollute the scents in the air.

"She definitely fell down 'ere, boss. I can smell her," Duggar said as he stood back up.

Rache strode over and crouched down, his nostrils flaring as he drew in whatever messages drifted on the air from the hole. He nodded. "Ah, yes, I can be smellin' her. Go get her."

Duggar's face contorted briefly with surprise, but he managed to stammer out, "Ya want me to follow after her down that? What if she died? What if it don't lead nowhere but death?"

"Yer not a pup, are ya? Actin' all scared of some chute down through the floor. I'm sure ya can do it, now get in there." Rache's voice was all business. He stood and turned to the other two.

"Stick, Spade, yer with me. We gonna go after that damnable Frog, Brunois. Any o' them side doors look promisin'?"

The two Mutts shifted back and forth. Spade finally nodded to the one on his left, saying, "I think that one be the best bet, boss."

Rache's gaze passed over them. It was fierce. He nodded and turned back to Duggar, who was still crouching by the hole, searching for an excuse not to go in.

"Well then, what'chya be waitin' fer Duggar?" Rache asked as he walked up closer to him.

"I, er, uh…just be decidin' the best way to climb down and start crawlin' through is all," Duggar replied.

A swift kick to his midsection sent Duggar tumbling headlong into the shaft beneath the floor. Rache withdrew his leg and crouched down to call into the tunnel.

"Duggar! Make certain ya find her, dead or alive. Alive be better so we can use her to bargain with if needs be, but dead be fine too, if that's the way she be when ya come upon her." Rache could hear his own voice echo as he sent it down the metal chute.

When he stood, Stick and Spade had already gathered the rest of their gear and opened the doorway. Rache began to sweep over the room a final time, making sure he did not miss anything. They hadn't found anything so far, but that didn't mean there wasn't anything to find.

Damn inbred Mutts couldn't find water if they fell out of a boat. Rache smirked a little at his own joke.

He stepped over Grimley's corpse without looking down at it. Not that he had an aversion to the dead; he just didn't find it worth the effort to look at the fallen Dog. An amorphous pool of red had seeped out from Grimley onto the ground.

Rache turned and walked back to the door where Stick and Spade stood. "Let's go, fellas. Ain't be nothin' else what worth takin' with us from this room."

A final flicker of the torchlight revealed a glint of something as they stepped through the doorway. Rache immediately turned and crouched to pick it up. It was a necklace with a tiny locket hung from it. There was nothing inside the locket, but the inscription on the back read, "To Rana, from Dad."

Rache tossed it about in his hand a few times and then tucked in into his jacket.

He rejoined the waiting Stick and Spade, and the three of them left into the serpentine tunnels of the complex. The going was slow. Unbearably slow at times for Rache. He channeled his frustration and annoyance into anger. His eyes bristled with crimson hatred.

I'll get that damn Frog yet. Oh yes, I'll get 'em.

CHAPTER

20

The field of metallic eggs sprawled through the cavern. Rana walked through it with great fear. The flame she kept in her hand cast orange and yellow light over the reflective surfaces of the structures as she walked. No two were identical, or at least no two that she saw. Some sprouted from the ground, others jutted from the walls, and still others hung from the ceiling like fat stalactites. Each of them had a cluster of tubes that went into their bases, all flowing from the same direction.

Rana followed them. She wasn't sure why she followed them. Something deep inside pulled her toward the source of all these things. Maybe it was a sense of adventure. Maybe it was destiny. Maybe it was delirium.

The tubes began to cluster into bigger tubes, which in turn fed into bigger ones still. She began to see circles of colored glass embedded into them and places where they entered massive boxes covered in dials and switches. Platforms and pathways appeared, allowing easier access to places that would have otherwise been difficult to reach.

Everything inside Rana told her something that looked like this should be bustling with activity, but only stillness prevailed. With each step, she expected to be assailed by some mechanical monstrosity or other abomination, but nothing stirred. She risked laying a hand on one of the tubes. It was as warm as the ambient temperature of the room, which was surprisingly so.

A faint light appeared in the distance. Or at least she thought it did.

Rana extinguished her own light and shut her eyes a moment. When she reopened them, she did indeed see a soft glow a way off. Her heart leapt at the prospect but immediately plummeted.

No telling what is making that light.

Nevertheless, she relit her own flame and continued on, stuffing down her fears and worries.

Her movement now was entirely upon the walkways that spanned over the sprawl of mechanisms and pipes. She was forced to walk carefully as they were without any sort of railing and rather poorly made. This made it especially difficult to navigate the stairs. When confronted with them, she would resort to crawling on all fours. Without a hand to hold her flame, she did so in the dark.

By the time she got to the third set of stairs, however, she no longer needed to supply her own light. The glow from whatever lay at the center of this strange complex was now strong enough to light her way. After a moment to steel her nerves and chastise her fears, she descended the stairs to a pathway in between two walls of pipes.

Rana reached out and knocked on one of the massive tubes with her fist. It bonged a long, hollow peal that echoed through the whole of the chamber. Nothing stirred.

A croak of frustration left her lips as she continued on, snaking her way along a path that wove in and out of the metal constructions. The strange light was dimmer in these odd trenches, but there was still enough of it for her to forego her own. Just because it was becoming easier to control the fire didn't mean it was without effort. Every little bit of energy mattered now.

The cramped pathway let out onto a clearing, full of the same tables and desks she had seen in the room she fell from. Some faced outward and some faced inward toward a giant sphere that sat on a pedestal in the middle. The floor was formed from many pieces of grating, all laid on top of support beams, and around the edge of the space were many glass columns, most of which were emitting light.

Amazing.

Rana edged her way over to the grated floor, still wary from her previous experience. Beneath her was a great sea of red, orange, and yellow, ebbing and flowing against unseen borders. The heat was even more palpable here than elsewhere, although not unbearable.

She tested the grate. First by attempting to wiggle it with her hand and, once satisfied, by gently placing her foot on it and slowly transferring weight, all the while holding onto a nearby pipe. It did not deposit her into the molten soup beneath.

She was thankful for that.

Fear quickly overtook her, though, when she saw the skeletons. There was a host of them. Some were

drooped over the equipment, others lay on the floor.
Many different Species could be seen among them. All
of them wore matching uniforms. She recognized the
colors and crest of the Fierchevals.

Soldiers?

Curiosity supplanted fear, and she began to walk
among them, searching for further clues. It was difficult
for her to look at them with the empty eye sockets of
the Cat, Dog, and Horse skulls staring at her. She did
her best not to look at the faces but was unsuccessful at
avoiding their gaze.

In the row closest to the center, there was a skeleton
whose clothing remnants were far nicer than the others.
Surmising it must be an officer, she forced herself to pat
it down, hoping to find something in its pockets. There
was a knife, a timepiece, a pipe, and a rotted billfold.

She took a deep breath, averted her eyes, and reached
within its jacket. The bones were dry and rough against
her skin as she fished around. Her fingers found something. It felt like a necklace. It took all her courage, but
she managed to reach behind the skeleton's head and
undo the clasp, turning away briskly once done.

The necklace was a simple chain with a locket on it.
She opened it to find a burnt piece of paper.

A photograph?

There was an inscription on the inside of the locket.
It read

Girard & Lola, Love Eternal

She tucked the locket into her pocket and turned
her attention to the sphere in the middle of the room.

It was a marvelous construction: clearly metallic but without seam or rivet. Leading into it from the ceiling of the cavern was a pipe that was several feet in diameter. Underneath it, another series of tubes went out beneath the grated floor and fed into the rest of the network Rana had navigated on her journey.

Whatever this place was, she had found the heart of it.

21

The curator of Dunham's Museum of Antiquities was exactly the stereotype Wourinos expected. He was a Mouse with brown fur, and wire-rimmed reading glasses worn low on his nose and secured around his neck with a thin cord.

"This is most unorthodox, Inspector. It is a rather late hour, you know." The curator looked every bit as annoyed as he sounded.

"I should think so, sir, but wholly warranted, I assure you," Wourinos replied, doing his best to play the political game.

The curator held some amount of influence in the city. He was a friend of the mayor and traveled in noble circles. Wourinos had known it would cost him something to gain access to the Mouse, and the museum, at this time of night.

"Well, anything I can do to help out the constabulary. Of course, I don't know what else there is to add to the statement I've already given. Do you have any news on how the case is progressing?" The curator's stare was hard for one so small.

"We have turned up some new information. The item was held for a short while by a fence in the city, but he has since had it stolen from him," Wourinos answered.

"Oh, well, serves him right, I suppose. Did this fence have a hand in the matter?"

"It's difficult to say, at this point, just how much his involvement was with the initial robbery. That is why I was hoping to learn more about the artifact itself to try and ascertain why the thieves would be fighting over it so, beyond the obvious reason of money."

The curator nodded. "Well, the artifact came from an old military collection that was deposited here toward the end of the Reformatory War. After it was stolen, I did some research and found that we actually had very little recorded information on it. That was probably one of the reasons it was stolen. As you well know, the thief had help from one of our custodial staff, a Dog named Kravitch. He had been assisting the assistant curator with sorting through the old military collection since it contained so many items of modest historical value that we were intending to sell to private collectors in order to free up some space. It was my assumption that while helping, he discovered the artifact and noted the lack of documentation on it and attempted to hide it for the theft later. In fact, had the assistant curator not gone back to check on something, it is likely no one would have noticed it was missing for a long time, if ever."

"So you have many things stored here that are not cataloged?"

"Of course not. Everything is *cataloged,* but until the Board of Directors gives me the assistance I require, there are many items that have insufficient details recorded. The end of the Reformatory War was a chaotic time. Many things that were in the possession of the military, but of a noncombat nature, were stored here. There are crates upon crates of unused uniforms and personnel records down there. "

Wourinos nodded as the curator spoke. It was nice to not have to pry information out of someone for a change. "Was there anything else stored with the artifact?"

An enthusiastic nod from the curator. He was clearly excited to be talking about his museum. "Yes, the artifact was stored among some other personal effects and was listed on the manifest as 'material evidence.' There is one item, in particular, that may be of interest to you."

Wourinos waited until he realized the curator was not going to continue without being asked. "And that item is?"

"A journal. A soldier's journal. In it, he describes the place where the artifact was found. It is quite an interesting read."

"May I see it then?"

"Of course, follow me." The curator turned and began walking down the hall.

Wourinos followed him to a set of stairs, and the pair descended them to the basement. At the bottom of the stairwell, the curator produced a key and unlocked a heavy oak door. The room they entered was massive and piled high with crates in many places. The curator turned on the gas lights, and they walked down a center aisle toward the back.

The amount of things stored was staggering to Wourinos. He considered himself a student of history and actually came to the museum quite often when he was not on the job. The various artifacts, relics, and other treasures of old drew his gaze as they went. There was a statue of Eshua, the Great Lion, that had to be several hundred years old. Wourinos stopped to admire it.

"Are you a religious fellow?" the curator asked him.

Wourinos shrugged. "You won't find me in the church often, but I believe."

"Even with all you must see? I should think that you often come into contact with the worst of what we are capable of."

Wourinos nodded without taking his eyes off the statue. "I do. But I also see where things should have gone very badly but didn't, and for no reason I can fathom. It makes me think there is hope for everyone. I choose to believe Animals can change." He turned to face the curator and said, "But until they do, I'll be there to stop them."

"A noble sentiment, Inspector." The curator resumed the walk down the aisle.

The journal was laid on a table at the back of the room. It was bound in simple brown leather and held shut with a piece of twine around a wooden knob.

The curator waved a hand at it and announced, "The journal of Sgt. Callum Bonne'Chance."

Wourinos raised an eyebrow at the name but said nothing.

The curator was too busy being theatrical to notice.

Wourinos picked the book up off the table, unwound the twine, and opened it. The pages were written in a sloppy but legible hand. He flipped through them, noting that some were missing toward the end and that nothing was written afterward.

"Yes, it would seem as if someone wished to keep something from that journal a secret," the curator stated.

"Do you know if the pages were present before the artifact was stolen?"

"I do not," the Mouse said, shaking his head. "I asked the same question of the assistant curator, and he could not confirm the condition of that book prior to the theft."

Wourinos nodded and placed the book within his jacket.

The curator began to protest, but Wourinos held up a paw and said, "I will return it once my investigation is complete."

The curator was not happy but did not argue. "Yes, well, just do be careful with it."

Wourinos grinned. He was always careful.

CHAPTER

22

From the journal of Callum Bonne'Chance:

June 6, 727 AE

I hate this damned place. I hate everything about it. Being stationed so close to the Wastes was bad enough, but now we have to make camp out in them just so we can meddle with things we shouldn't. I wish we had never found this damned door.

Each day they go a little deeper into the tunnels. They haven't brought anything out yet, but the lieutenant seems pretty excited at what they're finding. He called it a marvel. There's nothing marvelous about it. Isn't this sort of thing what threw the world into the Great Cataclysm?

They try to get me to accompany them, but I keep refusing. Someone has to stand guard, after all, and I'll be damned if they're going to drag me down into that place. Soon, they might not heed my protests, and the lieutenant will outright order me to go down and do one thing or another. I guess I'll have to then.

June 9, 727 AE

They brought more men from the main camp. Don't they know we have a war to fight? Half of our troop is now at these ruins. They've determined the interior of the tunnels to be safe, so now camp is in there. The new men brought supplies down in crates to one of the rooms. We're a good bit into them now.

I protested when they said we were moving, but the lieutenant just cut me off. Stupid bookworm from the city. He only has the post because his father knows someone else's father. I'd rather be out on the front where the Makivillaines are. That's where I would be if I hadn't broken that captain's nose. It still burns me up I'm the one that got punished when he's the one who took a swing at me. That's the army for you.

At least Kaile is here now. It's nice to have a friend. He's the only one I got in this place. I just wish he wasn't so excited about whatever it is they're fooling with further down. He comes back every night (or maybe day, it's hard to tell now that I can't see the sun), talking about everything they've been finding—giant metal eggs with some sort of constructs inside of them. He thinks that in time they will be able to bring them all to life. I tell him that is a horrible idea, but he doesn't listen.

I'm going to talk with the lieutenant again when I see him, and if he's not willing to give up this whole Svargan ruins business, I'm going to ask to be transferred out to another troop.

June 10, 727 AE

The lieutenant wouldn't listen to me. Stupid dandy. I tried to tell him that only bad would come from all of this, and we should just close the place up and be done with the whole affair. When he told me I was out of line, I requested transfer to another troop. He told me that he would not allow it. I hate him so very, very much.

June 13, 727 AE

Today, the lieutenant ordered me down to where they have been working. There was cluster upon cluster of metal egg-looking things, all of which had tubes and such running into them. They've found a central platform that has a big ball in the middle of it. This ball, they said, was what could bring all the things in the eggs to life. I didn't understand, nor did I want to.

The lieutenant is blind to all else. I don't think we've checked in with the main camp in four days now. His enthusiasm is really affecting Kaile. Every day, Kaile seems more and more willing to take foolish risks in trying to discover just what all of this stuff is and how it works. He even crawled under the platform that ball sits on to try and see how it works. He says that it takes the heat from the hot liquid rocks beneath and turns it into energy to power the creatures. I told him that sounded dangerous.

He said, "It would only be dangerous if there was a break in the valves under the platform that transmit the energy, and even then, only to those who were on the platform itself."

I told him that wasn't much comfort to me.

The lieutenant is happy with him though. He even let him take an egg, although he tells me it's not like the other ones but "an earlier version," whatever that means. He stores the thing where we bunk down. I do wonder what's inside of it though.

June 15, 727 AE

Kaile is dead. I told them nothing good would come of their meddling, and now, look, Kaile is dead! I could shoot the lieutenant right now. If it wasn't for his foolish notions of glory, none of this would have happened.

I was there when the thing attacked him. They had managed to bring one of the awful things to life. It was Kaile who had figured out how to do it by running a tube right from the ball to the egg. He was standing right next to it when the thing stood up. It had to be at least seven feet tall and had a bunch of arms. It took one look at Kaile and pounced on him, ripping him apart. It was more than I could bear, and I fired on it with everyone else who had their rifle doing likewise.

The lieutenant called out for us to stop, but we all just kept right on shooting. At first it didn't do much to the thing, but once we had all shot it five or six times, it went down. Damn thing took seven of us to bring it down.

Kaile's body was ordered topside, and I went with it. As I was leaving, I heard the lieutenant say, "It's a shame, but he was right. If we can figure out how to control them...."

Is he really going to try again to bring these things to life?

CHAPTER

23

Deeper still into the network of tunnels.

How much deeper could these things go? Auroka wondered.

The increasing warmth was becoming more noticeable as they went. It was not intolerable, but Brunois had unbuttoned the top of his jacket. Auroka found herself longing for a breeze. It didn't bother the Peste.

"I been wonderin''bout somethin'," Brunois said.

Auroka turned her head and glanced at him from the corner of her eye. "What's that?"

"Why you be doin' all this?" he asked her.

"What do you mean?"

"Well, I figure ya no havin' to be doin' this sort o' stuff. Ya say yer father knows th' inspector, so I reckon he probably be a man o' some importance. Yer clothin' be well made, and ya got some type o' proper trainin', so I figure all th' more so 'bout yer father. So iffn' he can be providin' all that fer ya, why ya be spendin' yer time out doin' this sort o' thing?"

Auroka nodded. She knew these questions would come eventually. She had not looked forward to it.

"Do you really think this is the time to discuss that?" She did her best to sound incredulous.

"Ya got somethin' else worth talkin' 'bout?"

"How about how we are going to find Rana and get out of here?"

"Well, fer now, we just gonna keep walkin' down this here tunnel, and since ya seem to put so much faith in the Peste, I guess it be leadin' th' way." Brunois looked at Auroka. "Well then, why ya be doin' this sort o' thing?"

Auroka sighed, recognizing she would not be able to deflect the Frog's questions.

"I do these things because I want to live my own life, not the life others tell me I am to live. I should be free to make my own choices." Her words had a rehearsed quality to them.

"And what do they be tellin' ya yer life ought to be like then?"

"Boring. A life of sitting and talking. Of having nice 'ladylike' pursuits and then getting married to just the right man for the good of the family. I can't even stand the thought of it."

Brunois laughed a little. "I don't be picturin' ya as the marryin' sort. Any man that would be wantin' to marry ya would have to be a brave one indeed."

Auroka smiled a little. "You have no idea."

The Peste came to a sudden halt and began to blink.

Brunois and Auroka stopped with it.

There was a glow up ahead. Faint, but there was definitely light.

They nodded to one another and drew their weapons as quietly as possible then began to walk toward it.

The Peste remained dark as they went; the slight buzz
he made was the only sound that could be heard.

Gradually, the glow grew to a light. The tunnel opened into a cavern. A cavern with metal walls,
floor, and ceiling—all of which were growing large
metal eggs.

Brunois and Auroka stopped and stared at the sprawl
of mechanical forms that filled the space. The eggs, the
tubes that fed into them, the boxes, and the walkways
that crossed about the great web of metal constructs. It
was incredible.

"Place look to be some sort o' hive," Brunois said.

The Peste blinked a single time.

"This where ya come from?" Brunois asked the Peste.

The Peste blinked twice.

"I think that means no," Auroka offered.

Brunois nodded.

The three of them began to travel down the main
pathway. All around them were stairwells and side paths
that led into the clusters of eggs and tubes. At times, the
solid floor would turn to metal grating, beneath which
could be seen rivers of molten rock, glowing orange and
red as they flowed along.

"This is why these caverns are so warm. The whole
place must be part of some sort of deep fissure,"
Auroka stated.

Brunois nodded but wasn't really paying attention.
His gaze was focused on a structure further off from
where they stood. There was a great tube coming from
the top of it, but he couldn't see the rest of it past all of
the other machinery.

"Ya be noticin' how all these pipes and such lead back in the same direction?" he asked Auroka.

She nodded. "That's not too surprising. It makes sense there would be a central point to all of this."

"I think that be it," Brunois said and pointed to the tall structure he had been studying.

"Yes, I think so too."

"I also be thinkin' that if Rana fell through some vent and ended up down here, that probably be the way she head. She'd have been seein' the light o' this place same as we did and make sense she'd go to it."

"That seems likely."

Their pace quickened.

The Peste stayed close to them as they went. It kept itself unlit and hovered near Brunois as if it were trying to hide.

Auroka took note of its odd behavior and asked, "Do you think the Peste is scared? It won't leave your side."

Brunois looked up at his flying companion.

It looked back at him and then landed on his shoulder.

Brunois made no move to swat it away. He did croak a little though as he turned his head back to face the direction they were walking.

Auroka smiled. "Awww, he's growing on you."

"Like a wart," Brunois croaked back.

"I thought Frogs like warts?"

Brunois snorted. "Yer thinkin' of Toads, missy."

Despite his grumbling, there was something that felt good about the little brass firefly that rested on his shoulder. He'd be damned if he would admit it though.

They came closer to the center of the mechanical hive. The tubes that ran in from the outer edges were clustered into great banks, too tall for them to see over. What had been a pathway was now a corridor, walled in by stacks of pipes.

The machinery around them was silent, but the flow of magma below their feet moaned and gurgled. It was just loud enough to mask the sound of the Dogs not far behind them.

CHAPTER

24

Rana studied the sphere in the center of the clearing and the pedestal on which it sat. She tapped it with her knuckles. It sounded hollow, but not entirely so. The pedestal gave way to a column, which went down into the sea of magma below.

Why doesn't it melt in that heat?

She noticed several switches where the whole thing met the grated floor. The temptation took her in, and she flipped one. A dull whirr drifted up from beneath her, followed by a clank. She tried another switch with the same result. Then all of them.

I probably shouldn't be meddling with any of this.

It felt good to be doing *something* though. To take some control of the situation around her instead of being pushed along through it. Whatever secrets this place held, she was determined to find out. Even though she could not stay here long, she would come back. She would discover them.

"Don't move." The voice was a Dog's.

Rana froze.

"Put your hands up above your head and then turn around real slow," it continued in a gruff bark.

She did as she was told, fear welling up in her again. Her heartbeat rose. She began to get tunnel vision.

"There's a good girl then." The Dog had a rifle aimed at her. "Now walk over there."

Rana began to walk over toward the pathway the Dog indicated, but then dove behind one of the consoles. A bullet pinged off the metal grating nearby. She conjured a ball of fire and threw it back at him.

No, not this time. This time, I fight.

Her blood rushed to her head. Two more shots struck the console behind her. Rana blindly threw more fireballs at where she thought the Dog might be.

He called out, "Don't be stupid, little girl! Ain't no need for you to die here. You can come through all of this alive, just give up."

Anger displaced her fear. It was hot and seared her insides. Everything began to turn to red, and she swore she was going to burst into flames.

Beneath the grated floor, the sea of magma churned. The sphere in the center of the platform shook. The consoles came to life, lights flashing across them.

Throughout the mechanical hive, pipes began to rattle. Metal gears clanked and valves popped. A great cacophony of unnatural noises clicked, chattered, and buzzed to life.

The hive had awoken.

Black shapes filled the space of the cavern, swirling in a large mass, which continued to grow. Their chittering and chattering drowned out all other sounds as it echoed off the walls. Flashes of light rippled through the swarm, reflecting off the metal surfaces of the individual members.

Rana gaped. Then she ran. She didn't even give a thought as to whether or not the Dog would shoot her when she stepped out from her cover. She just ran.

Duggar ran too. He rolled out from behind the console he had been hiding behind and bounded off in the same direction as Rana. The skeletons impeded his ability to run, their sprawled forms littering the platform, threatening to trip him. He leapt up onto a console and began jumping from one to another, seeking to avoid the piles of bones.

A metal form descended from the swarm and snatched him in midair.

He screamed in the howling way unique to a Dog whose life is about to end.

Rana looked over her shoulder as she ran. She saw rapidly moving limbs hovering in the air, some metal, some furry. The furry ones began to fall to the ground.

She faced forward again and ran with a vigor she had not known she possessed. All around her, eggs continued to open. Shiny appendages poked out, followed by glass-eyed heads and winged bodies. They left their pods and joined the mechanical gyre. She fought back the paralyzing terror and kept running.

Duggar's final yowl gurgled through the whirring of the swarm's ascension. It tinged Rana's bones with a primal, twisting sensation.

The lights dimmed as she ran further from the central platform. She stumbled and crashed nose-first to the ground. The pain didn't come close to penetrating the surge of adrenaline in her body. She got her feet under her again and continued to run.

She turned a corner in the pathway, which brought two forms and a blip of light into view. Brunois, Auroka, and the Peste. They just stood there, staring.

Why aren't they running? Don't they see what's going on?

Rana bolted right past them and kept on moving, hollering out "Run!" as she did. She wasn't going to stop, but she did turn her head enough to see if they were moving.

They were. The Frog and the Horse had been shaken from their reverie when Rana had crashed past them. Now both of them mustered their strength and ran, the Peste flying alongside them.

Auroka, being more suited to running, closed the distance between her and Rana first and exclaimed, "Thank heaven you're alive!"

"Ain't none o' us gonna be alive fer long iffn' we don't get ourselves out o' this place double quick!" Brunois's voice was loud but strained from his exertion. Frogs just weren't as natural a bunch of runners as Horses.

"So run!" Rana croaked back, not stopping her own mad dash for safety.

Brunois came alongside her. "Ya be all right, Rana?"

Auroka had already disappeared around a turn in the tunnel.

"For now!" she called back.

Brunois just nodded. There was no more time for words. Only running.

They came around the bend in the tunnel.

"Over here! Get down!" Auroka yelled out to them.

Brunois dove to the right, rolling behind an instrument panel to join Auroka.

Rana leapt the other direction. There was nothing for her to roll behind, so she skittered along the rounded wall of the tunnel.

Gunfire erupted from further up the corridor.

Brunois and Auroka crouched behind their cover and readied their weapons. The Peste stayed close to Brunois, blinking erratically.

Rana had no choice but to scramble for cover behind a rock. The distance between her and her companions seemed insurmountable. Bullets whizzed through the gulf that separated them.

The buzzing from behind intensified.

The swarm was coming.

25

Brunois cocked his revolvers and returned fire, taking in the scene as he shot. It was grim. The Dogs were entrenched behind a wide bank of instruments a hundred feet from where they now hid. On the opposite wall, halfway up the tunnel, Rana cowered behind a rock. There was no other cover.

He reloaded his revolvers, snapped the break shut, and looked over to Auroka. "I'm gonna try and get Rana."

Auroka drew her bow. A shimmering arrow of light crackled into existence. She loosed it at the back of the tunnel where it struck a metal creature resembling a wasp bigger than she was. It contorted in a spasm and fell to the ground twitching. Another arrow struck it, and it went still.

"We need to get out of here," Auroka said as she drew her bow again. "If we stay here, those things will devour us."

Gunshots struck the metal panel they crouched behind. More hit the floor and walls of the tunnel.

Bleedin' trapped, Brunois lamented.

He turned to Auroka and said, "Yer right, be ready to go."

The Peste flew down next to his face.

"I need ya to be gettin' up there and distract them Dogs. Iffn' they be shootin' at ya, we might be havin' a chance to get past 'em."

The Peste blinked once and took off toward the Dogs, flying in arcs and swoops, light blazing.

Rana saw it go and peeked her head out into the tunnel. She saw where the Dogs were and began throwing fireballs at them. Tongues of red, orange, and yellow flame rolled across the walls and metal panels of their refuge.

That's m'girl, Brunois grinned inwardly at the sight of the fire.

Auroka's arrows flew in a steady stream of light toward the back of the tunnel. The insectile constructs kept coming. The smoking husks of the downed ones piled up, their forms twitching in brief fits of final exertion. The heap of their lifeless shells helped to bottleneck the opening to the tunnel, but the live ones just pushed through them and kept coming.

Brunois rolled out from his cover and fired twice, then took off up the tunnel. Up ahead, he saw Rana's dancing flames, and the Peste's swirling light. He charged straight at them, continuing to shoot at the Dogs.

"Follow me!" he called to Rana as he passed her.

She joined him, continuing to assault the Dogs with a barrage of fire.

Behind them, Auroka continued to fire into the rear maw of the tunnel as she moved backward towards the Frogs. The mass of metal appendages was now so great that she could no longer pick out individual members of it. So she just kept firing.

Bullets flew in erratic directions, trying to hit the Peste. The little firefly buzzed and weaved in between the Dogs, who were cowering from the increasing inferno that Rana unleashed upon them.

Auroka turned and ran up alongside the Frogs, foregoing further shots at the insect horde. The three of them ran past the Dogs, firing at them as they went.

The swarm was not far behind.

Rache, Stick, and Spade turned to fire at the escaping group. Rache shot at Brunois. Spade shot at Auroka. Stick was crushed beneath a gnashing set of metal limbs.

The metal insect tore into the Dog, ripping and slashing at his body. Fur flew, bits of flesh and bone attached to it. Stick bellowed a strained howl of gruesome agony, which was quickly supplanted by wet, snapping sounds.

Rache and Spade clamored backward in horror, the rifles in their hands forgotten. They ran after Brunois and his party.

Rocks and dips in the tunnel floor made it difficult to run. Auroka strode over the obstacles with ease, but it was not so easy for Brunois and Rana. The two Frogs struggled to keep pace with their companion, tripping and stumbling often as they fought their way through the debris that littered their path. The Peste didn't have any trouble at all, but he did remain close to Brunois and Rana, lighting the way for them.

The awakening of the swarm had also brought to life a limited amount of lighting in the subterranean complex. Circles of glass at regular intervals bathed the tunnels in an orange glow. It was enough light to navigate by, but only barely so, and the additional illumination supplied by the Peste was welcome.

Rana began to fall behind. Running against the upward slope of the tunnel had rapidly consumed what little energy she had. She struggled for breath. The hot air was unsatisfying to her hungry lungs. It had a metallic taste that caused her jaw to clench.

The Peste swooped in front of Brunois and alerted him to Rana. He turned to see her slowing.

"C'mon, Rana! You can make it. Don't be givin' up on me!" he yelled down to her as he hopped back a few steps.

She collapsed against him, and Brunois called out, "Auroka! We need some help down 'ere!"

Brunois helped his niece back to her feet, and they started up the tunnel again. They turned a corner and arrived at a landing with many tunnels leading off in different directions. Auroka stood at the base of it, scanning the different openings.

"Which way do we be goin' then?" Brunois asked.

The Peste was the first to respond, flying over to a tunnel on their right and blinking.

Auroka turned to help the Frogs but was interrupted by two furry blurs that slammed into them. Everyone but the Peste crashed to the floor.

The clawing, buzzing peal of the swarm echoed into the chamber as some of the metal insects flew out of the tunnel. Everyone rolled out of the way. Brunois, Auroka, and the Peste on one side; Rana, Rache, and Spade on the other.

Everyone opened fire with whatever they had at their disposal. Bullets bit into the shiny forms, causing strange fluids to begin spewing out. Flashes of light and blooms of fire erupted within the mass of mechanisms as Auroka and Rana attacked. Insectile constructs began to fall to the ground, but the fury of the swarm continued to pour into the space, a growing column that separated the two groups.

Each had no choice but to flee into the tunnels available to them.

"Rana!" Brunois yelled as Auroka grabbed him by the collar and jerked him into the tunnel.

"You can't help her now! We'll have to find her when we get out of this mess!"

"Rache'll kill 'er!" he croaked back, struggling against her grip.

"No, he won't. He needs her to help fight back so they can escape. We'll find her when we get topside." Auroka's tone was commanding, her stare unflinching.

Brunois reluctantly turned, and the pair of them chased after the Peste, who was lighting their escape route.

26

Her fireballs were not as effective against the mechanical insects as she would have liked. It was all she had, though, so she continued to launch them at the column stretching across the center of the room. She began to back away along with the two Dogs.

Rache and Spade continued to fire into the swarm, reloading their rifles as they went. Were it not for Rana's more substantial firepower, the three of them would have been rent asunder.

When they reached the threshold of the tunnel, Rana conjured a great wave of flame and sent it surging toward the swarm. She hoped it would be enough. With some distance now in between the three of them and the insects, they all turned and ran.

A flame sprang to life in Rana's hand, helping to light the way as they went. The Dogs were much faster and very quickly outpaced her. But she kept running. Exhaustion threatened to lay her down with every stride. But she kept running. Her lungs screamed and her legs wailed. But she kept running.

She came out onto another landing, to find the Dogs already there and pondering which route to take.

The sound of the swarm was not far behind, and when she turned, she could see the mechanical forms creeping their way up the tunnel.

Rana conjured another massive wave of fire and sent it crashing down upon them. She fell to her knees immediately afterward. A hissing sound, coupled with a few muffled explosions, let her know her exertions had not been in vain.

"Get yerself up there, missy, we be needin' ya," Rache said. He stood next to Rana and pulled her to her feet.

Rana winced a little at the pain but knew that she did need to keep moving.

Even if it means with them.

Her emotions were hot and raw inside her but indistinct from the adrenaline. She raised her hands, and with them, the conflagration in the tunnel below elevated in strength. It was now a blazing inferno.

Rache stepped back from the searing heat that funneled upward from the mouth of the tunnel. It singed his fur slightly. He pulled Rana around.

"Let's go," he barked. "Yer first, missy."

"My name is Rana, not missy," she retorted.

"Yer name is 'bout to be dead Frog iffn' ya don't start movin' up that tunnel there." Rache pushed her toward one of the openings and waved Spade along with them.

Rana conjured a small flame for light, and the three of them began to move.

"Hurry up!" Rache growled at her and poked her in the back with the barrel of his rifle.

The impact of the metal between her shoulder blades sent a jolt of pain down Rana's spine. The flame in her hand grew brighter and hotter. She quickened the pace to a jog, although she knew she could not keep it up for long.

They came to another landing, with more choices, and took the only tunnel that had an upward slope to it. It was difficult to tell how far down they had gone initially, and how far up they had come since fleeing the swarm. Rana felt as if they had been down here for years.

"Ya feel that?" Rache asked Spade.

"Feel what?" he asked back.

"It ain't so bleedin' hot anymore. We must be getting close. Air startin' to smell fresher too." Rache grinned a little, his white fangs glistening in Rana's reddish "torchlight."

The thought of fresh air and sunlight spurred them onward. Especially Rana.

As soon as we hit sunlight, torch them as hard as you can, then run.

She drew strength from this thought, even though the prospect of doing it frightened her, even though it made her cringe at the notion of taking a life.

The doorway appeared, offering temporary respite, if not salvation, from the industrial abominations below. All three ran up to it and searched for a way to pry it open. Its seams were perfectly fitted and would require tools to be parted.

Rache pounded on it with his fists and cursed bitterly and for a long time.

Rana turned from the door and began to search the consoles and panels around it, hoping for some way of opening it.

The Peste had to have switched something when it opened the other door...

Buzzing and clanking sounds began to drift up through the tunnel. The two Dogs and Rana exchanged a fearful look.

"There has to be something here to open the door. Help me find it." Rana surprised herself with the tone of her voice.

Rache nodded. "Start lookin', Spade."

There was little to be seen on the panels themselves, mosty dials. What few switches there were they flipped, but to no avail. Having found nothing, Rana turned her attention to the frame of the door.

The buzzing and clanking intensified.

Rana's eyes caught a button halfway up the door-frame. She smashed her hand on it. Her heart raced.

More buzzing from below.

If we don't get this door open, we're dead.

A sharp click echoed in the small space, replaced by a faint whirring as the door began to open. Fresh air poured in, carrying moonlight with it. Rana had never tasted anything so good in all her life.

The two Dogs immediately leapt through the door and disappeared to either side.

Rana pushed the button a second time. There was a loud clang of gears grinding, and then the door began to close. She hopped through the opening before it did.

The moon and the stars above were as jewels glistening in paradise, even out in the Wastes as they were. They had escaped and sealed the door behind them.

I doubt it will hold them forever. But long enough to get away.

She looked about, trying to orient herself. Rache and Spade were nowhere in sight. Even though she had no idea where she was or which direction she should go, she started running. Any place was better than here.

Spade stepped into view, rifle raised.

Rana raised her hands to conjure a fireball and then everything went black as a sudden pain erupted at the base of her skull.

CHAPTER

27

Anger and fear coursed through Brunois in equal measure. It was difficult for him to distinguish which emotion was directed at the swarm and which stemmed from Rana now being with Rache. Maybe there was no distinction to be made. Emotions are messy.

Regardless, both spurred him upward through the tunnel, trailing behind Auroka and the Peste. Behind them, the mechanical swarm continued to churn and writhe, following them toward the surface. Brunois was running low on ammunition, and after considering how many bullets it took to fell one of those things, he decided his efforts were best put to running for his life.

The Peste was a faithful guide and brought them back to the door they had locked. Auroka spun the wheel, opened it, and the pair darted through. They didn't give a second look to the body of the Dog Brunois had shot earlier; they just leapt over it and kept on running after the Peste.

They wound upward through the tunnels that they had descended only hours before. When they reached the gaslights, their pace quickened. Escape from this horrid place was within their reach. They pounded and bounded toward the surface, desperate to escape the monsters below.

Moonlight greeted them when they arrived at the entryway. The doorway was still propped open by the rock Auroka had placed there. The Peste sailed through the gap into the night, followed by Auroka and Brunois, who had to turn sideways to squeeze through.

Auroka yanked the rock out of the doorway. It slid shut with a relieving clank.

They turned to each other, the Peste hovering nearby.

"I feel better 'bout gettin' more distance between us and this place, but we need t'find what happen'd to Rana first," Brunois said.

Auroka nodded. "In my exploration of this place before, I had found other doors. This was just the closest from the outpost. There is another not far."

"That's where we be goin' then."

Auroka nodded and started to run further into the Wastes, Brunois beside her and the Peste flying by his shoulder. The moon was full and supplied plenty of light to run by from its place in the cloudless sky. The air was crisp and tasted of hope.

They arrived at a rocky outcropping after a few minutes of running. It looked much the same as the other, a low hill with steel doors bearing a firefly insignia.

Auroka held up a fist, and Brunois slowed to a stop. She motioned the Peste over and pointed at the ground, asking it, "Light?"

It blinked once and glowed steadily, shining its light on the ground just outside the door.

Auroka bent down to study the dirt. "They came out here."

Brunois's heart hopped inside his chest.

"Two Dogs and Rana," she continued, moving away from the door, face close to the ground. "They scattered when they came out, Rana ran along this path. She fell over here, and then there's no more of her tracks."

"Ya think they killed 'er?" Brunois asked, the fear in his voice plain.

Auroka shook her head. "No, because her body isn't here. If they killed her, it seems unlikely they would carry her along. They probably knocked her out so she wouldn't cause trouble and are now carrying her with them."

"There be more tracks of the Dogs to follow?"

Auroka nodded and began to lead the party after the Dogs.

The Peste provided plenty of light, and the tracks were easy to see. The Dogs were making no attempt to conceal their passing, just fleeing in terror. Their path led back the way they had entered the Wastes.

"Can't we be goin' any faster?" Brunois croaked.

"No," Auroka snapped back at him. "We have to pace ourselves so we can keep moving once they stop. They're tough, but they also have Rana to carry. Once they reach some of the Rebirthed Lands, I think they'll take some time to rest. That will be our chance."

Brunois nodded at the sense of that, but he didn't like it.

Hang in there, Rana, he willed to her across the distance.

Rock by rock, the landscape changed from completely barren to clumps of sickly looking vegetation. These small bastions of life multiplied as they moved further across the boundary between the Wastes and the Rebirthed Lands. By sunrise, grasses had begun to appear, and the pair had crossed a brook that might possibly be drinkable.

Brunois stopped and waved the Peste over to him. It came. "Time to be windin' ya there." He held out his hand, and once it landed, he wound the little brass firefly and placed him to sit on his shoulder.

"The tracks lead off that way," Auroka said, pointing westward. "But Jahn's outpost is not far to the north. We should stop there for supplies and to tell him of what's happened."

"But Rana may no have time fer such breaks! We need to keep followin' them."

Auroka leveled her stare at him with all the authority she could muster, which was substantial. "We also have to consider that swarm. Someone needs to know; the Royal Army must be alerted. If it breaks out of that hive, there's no telling what it might do. If Rache kills us, then no one will know until it's too late. We have a duty to the rest of the kingdom."

"Maybe you do, but my only duty be t'Rana." His voice wavered. There was fear in it, intermingled with hatred and anger.

Auroka nodded. "Then you go on your own. I'm going to tell Jahn what happened. You can follow them if you want, but I don't think you'll be able to track them without me."

Brunois's faced contorted in a mixture of rage and despair. He nodded. "Let's be quick about it then."

Jahn was out among the shanties when the three of them arrived.

"Well, good morning there!" he called out to them. "Welcome back!"

As they got closer, Jahn could make out their disheveled forms and smaller number. His countenance dropped.

"Are you all right?" he asked.

"No, Jahn, we are not. But time is short right now. We need water and rations, and Brunois needs ammunition. If you don't have any that'll fit his revolvers, he'll need whatever firearms you have. Then I need you to make ready and start heading west for Dunham." Her voice was commanding.

Jahn simply nodded and asked, "What do you need me to go there for?"

"The ruins we went to explore, the ones with the insect symbol on the doors, you know where they are?" she asked back.

Jahn nodded.

"We found something awful in them," she continued, graveness permeating her tone. "A huge swarm of mechanical insects. It's awake. We think we trapped it in there, but it may break out. Alert the constabulary in Dunham, tell them to contact the Royal Army."

Jahn stared back at her.

Brunois shifted as he watched the exchange, the Peste flickering a few times on his shoulder.

"That sounds like quite a story…." Jahn finally said. "I'm not saying I don't believe you, but I'm not so certain they'll believe me."

Auroka nodded and reached inside her vest. She withdrew a ring and handed it to Jahn, saying, "Give that to Inspector Wourinos and use my name. Make him believe."

Jahn took the ring and bowed. "As you command then, Lady Fiercheval."

Brunois blinked.

So did the Peste, but it was in response to Brunois's reaction.

The Frog stared at Auroka. "You're a Fiercheval?"

She nodded. "Now, let's get our supplies and find Rana."

CHAPTER

28

Brunois did his best to keep up with Auroka. The Horse moved through the woodlands so easily, even while tracking Rache. He managed though.

The Peste was ahead of both of them.

Little bugger is out scoutin' fer us. Brunois actually laughed a little at that thought.

The path they traversed was not a clear one, cutting straight through the more difficult parts of the terrain. Brunois was forced to leap, hop, and scuttle over all manner of rock, ditch, and fallen tree. The exertion was tiring out his already exhausted body. But onward he went, desperate to overtake Rache.

I'm comin', Rana.

Up ahead, he saw Auroka come to a stop and crouch, the blinking light of the Peste hovering near her. Brunois slowed his pace enough to silence his footfalls. He bent low as he walked up next to her, trying to even out his breathing.

"Ya find her?" he asked as softly as possible.

Auroka nodded and said, "Yes, but it's not good."

His heart fell from his chest into his stomach. He stared down from the hill they sat atop. It looked like someone had started to build a fire.

"No one's there," he said to Auroka.

"You see the wood stacked up? They were about to settle down and rest, but now they aren't there. I think they heard or saw our approach," she whispered back.

"Where did they go?"

"Not far."

"Step out from yer cover, I know ya be there! I'll kill 'er if ya don't." Rache's bark was unmistakable.

Auroka laid a hand on Brunois's arm and shook her head, silently mouthing, "Not yet."

"I know ya be up there! That flyin' light gave ya 'way. Now be showin' yerselves or I be splittin' little miss Rana's head open!"

Brunois looked to Auroka and said, "He's gonna kill 'er! I'm goin' down."

"He won't kill her until he's certain we're here, and where we are," she replied.

"Ain't a chance I be willin' to take. He don't know you be here, so maybe if I go down, you can get the drop on 'em." Without waiting for her reply, he stood and began to walk down the hillside.

"I'm comin' down!" Brunois called out, hands held above his head.

Spade appeared from behind a tree when Brunois reached the base of the hill. He moved out to the Frog and removed the gun belt from his waist and the sword from his back.

"What ya be wantin', Rache?" Brunois croaked.

"I want to be knowin' where that Horse is hidin' at," Rache barked back.

"Bugs got 'er," Brunois said, trying to pin down the direction Rache's voice was coming from.

"That be a damn shame. Ya don't seem too broken up 'bout it," Rache barked again.

"What do I be carin', she was just th'guide," Brunois retorted. "Ya got m'guns. Let Rana go, and you can just be walkin' away."

Rache stepped out from behind a tree, Rana in front of him, bound, gagged, and with a gun to her head. "But you and I still got business what needs settlin'. You killed a few o' my boys, ya know."

Brunois looked Rana over. Fear shone in her eyes, but she did not appear hurt. Her hands were bound behind her back, and a neckerchief ran through her mouth as a gag.

"Fine, take me, let her go." Brunois finally said to Rache.

Rache snarled. "No, I think I'm gonna be killin' ya both. Real question be, who goes first. Her…"

He pressed the gun into Rana's head. She winced.

"Or you."

He pointed the gun at Brunois.

A few feet away, a flash of light exploded as Spade was sent hurtling through the air. Auroka had hit her mark.

Brunois dove off to the side, knowing a shot would be coming from Rache.

It did come, but it was wild and accompanied by a great howl.

Brunois looked up to see Rana running and Rache burning. The Dog dropped to the ground and patted at the flames until they were extinguished.

The rapier Spade had taken from Brunois had been tossed just as far as the Dog himself when he was struck by Auroka's arrow. It lay a few feet from where Brunois stood. He dove at it, picking it up and unsheathing it as he rolled to his feet.

Rache had regained his feet and drew a sword of his own. A massive, cruel implement as long as Brunois was tall.

The Canine's fur was burned away at the abdomen. The smell of it was awful in the air. He rounded on Brunois, sword raised, snarl plastered across his muzzle.

"I'm gonna kill ya, Frog," Rache growled. The sound was primal and full of carnage.

"Then quit yer talkin' and get to it," he croaked back.

His goad worked. Rache swung at Brunois.

The Frog ducked and stepped back. There were times when being small had its advantages.

A nearby tree was unfortunate enough to have grown in that spot and was split in two. The top portion fell between the combatants. Rache leapt over it, swinging his sword over his head.

Brunois sidestepped and parried but was too far away to strike back.

The Dog spun around and swung again.

Another step and parry from Brunois.

Up on the hill, Auroka watched the two combatants, bow drawn, arrow bristling with energy between her fingers. She searched for the clear shot, but they were too close to one another and moving too fast for her to fire safely.

Rache bellowed out a feral howl and lunged again.

Brunois sidestepped and parried, countering with his own thrust. He stuck Rache in the shoulder of his off hand.

The steel puncture didn't even faze Rache. He kicked Brunois in the midsection and sent him flying through the air, the Frog's sword being pulled from Rache's shoulder as he went.

After hitting the ground and trying to roll back to his feet, Brunois croaked and wheezed, the air having gone out of him. His wind was slow in coming back.

Rache seized the opportunity and charged forward. His sword flashed in the light of the forest. He would have the Frog this time.

Steel met steel. With not enough breath in him to move out of the way, all Brunois could do was get his sword in between Rache's and his own body. The force bowled him over and knocked the sword from his hand.

The kill was Rache's. The massive black Dog circled around and raised his sword, ready to cleave Brunois where he lay.

The sword descended but did not hit its mark.

Fire roared to life on the Dog's body. It engulfed him. Anguished howls echoed through the woods; they were Rache's final words as the immolation overtook him. His form fell to the ground, continuing to burn.

Rana lowered her shaking hands. She stared at Rache's body as the flames died down to a smolder.

Brunois joined her, laying a hand on her shoulder but saying nothing.

It took Rana several minutes to become aware of anything. Her own shock had overwhelmed her; she had never taken a life. When she did snap out of her daze, she turned to her uncle and buried her head in his chest. Tears.

Somewhere deep inside, Brunois found some fatherly instinct and wrapped his arms around his sobbing niece.

"It be all right, Rana. Yer safe 'gain. I gotchya," he said to her. Compassion filled his words.

The Peste joined the family reunion, landing on Brunois's shoulder and blinking in a consoling fashion. Brunois gave it a glance and smiled, then he squeezed Rana a little harder.

"Are you hurt, Rana?" Auroka asked as she walked up on the three of them. She had collected Brunois's gun belt and revolvers on her way.

Brunois made no move to take them. He just hugged his niece.

"I'm all right," Rana managed to say as her tears subsided.

Auroka nodded and laid a hand on her back. "Good."

Their moment of reunion was interrupted by the Peste taking off back to the top of the hill. It blinked furiously.

Rana, Brunois, and Auroka all shared a look and then went up to see. Silence hung between them as the icy grip of fear clamped down on their hearts. Each wore an ashen face by the time they reached the hill's crest. They gazed out toward the Wastes.

A gray cloud grew on the horizon. The swarm was loose.

CHAPTER

29

"We need to alert the army," Auroka said. "That swarm must be stopped."

No one disagreed.

Out on the horizon, the swarm was swelling, a seething gray mass of metallic insects.

"Isn't that what ya sent Jahn t'do?" Brunois asked.

"Yes. But it's out now. If the army can't contain it, or destroy it, there's no telling where it might go or what it might do."

"So we off fer Dunham then?"

Auroka sighed. "Yes, we have to try. Although, even at the fastest pace I alone can muster, it will take several days." She stared out at the growing amorphous shape. "And I think it is headed this way. It will overtake us, if it is."

"I have an idea," Rana said. "We can go back to the outpost...."

"Go back toward the bleedin' things?" Brunois interrupted. "Nothin' doin', Rana. Who knows, they may no even follow us if we just bugger off from 'ere."

Auroka put a hand on Brunois's arm, silencing him. She looked over to Rana and asked, "What's your idea?"

"The flying machine," Rana proudly announced.

"But Jahn said it doesn't work, Rana," Auroka replied.

Brunois chimed in. "Yeah, remember he sayin' it be too heavy once we put th'fuel in it…"

Rana grinned. "But we're not going to use fuel. I'll heat the boiler myself."

Two nods, and a single blink, came from her companions.

"All right then. Let's go," Auroka said.

They gathered up what little gear they still had and began to trek back toward the outpost. Legs screamed, joints ached, feet protested with every step, but they kept walking. None of them enjoyed the idea of walking back into the swarm, but they had all agreed it was what they had to do.

Jahn was still at the outpost when they arrived, making final preparation for his journey, and quite hastily at that. A distant buzz was escalating—an ill omen. It carried with it a sense of dread that Brunois and his party knew far better than any of them cared to. Even Jahn was on edge as they walked up to him.

"Ah, glad to see you were able to rescue Ms. Rana." His voice was polite but strained with anxiety. "And not that it isn't always good to see you, but I must ask, what are you doing here? Do you not hear that awful sound they are making?"

"The flying machine, what does it need to be ready to fly other than fuel for the boiler?" Auroka asked Jahn.

The Mule balked at the question but regained his wits and replied, "I suppose just to check if it has enough water in it and that the moving parts are lubricated."

"How long will that take if we help?"

Jahn shrugged a little and answered, "Maybe half an hour?"

"Then let's get started. Where is the lubricant?" Auroka had made up her mind, and everyone else seemed to be falling in line.

Jahn produced an oil can from within one of the shanties and pointed toward a few water barrels. They all set to work preparing the machine. Jahn checked the water level, which was none, and poured several barrels of water in. Auroka and Rana lubricated and inspected the moving parts, leaving the Peste and Brunois to stow the gear, a task largely completed by Brunois.

Preparations made, they boarded.

"Who be steerin' this thing?" Brunois asked. "Don't know nothin' 'bout this sort o' thing m'self."

"I'll steer," Rana said, her voice even as she spoke.

The rest of them stared at her. Jahn began to protest but decided not to. They all gave each other wary looks.

It was Auroka who spoke first. "You think you can handle it?"

Rana nodded. "Yes, I think so. What choice do we have?"

Another round of nods from the rest of the party, accompanied by a single blink from the Peste.

"Easy fer you to say," Brunois croaked at the Peste. "You can just fly away iffn' the whole thing come crashing down."

They all boarded the flying machine and sat in their respective spots. There were harnesses attached to the benches, and everyone strapped in.

Up front, Rana buckled herself into the captain's chair and put her hand on the controls. "Jahn?" she called out.

"Yes?"

"This thing have a name?"

"Folks who brought it called it an Ornithopter, I think. It's been a while."

"Ornithopter?" Rana asked back.

"Ornithopter," Jahn confirmed.

"That's a horrible name," Rana said as she closed her eyes.

She pictured the boiler in her mind. The shell of it, the chamber now filled with water, the base of it where a fire would ordinarily be lit. Her breathing became even as she focused, gradually becoming deeper and deeper. The boiler began to shimmy.

Wheels began to turn on the sides of it, powering hydraulic arms attached to the wings. Slowly at first, they made a full rotation.

The wings rose and fell.

The wheels turned faster.

The wings rose and fell again, the Ornithopter hopping slightly.

The wheels began to spin steadily.

The wings beat the air in an even rhythm.

The Ornithopter left the ground and rose above the trees.

Rana continued to focus on the boiler, heating it as much as she could. Her experience on the train came back to her. It had only been a few weeks ago; it felt like it had been a lifetime ago. She felt like a different Frog from who she had been then. This time, she would control her gift; this time, she wouldn't let her fear overcome her.

She pitched the control stick forward and started off.

"Rana! The other way!" Auroka shouted and tried to point westward.

The metal contraption and its occupants were headed toward the swarm. The churning mass of metal was about a mile off, with a few of the mechanical insects much closer and flying right at them.

Rana rolled the Ornithopter to the right and began to turn, putting the afternoon sun at her nose. Her concentration was absolute as she kept her mind focused on both heating the boiler and piloting the aircraft.

Gunfire erupted from the belly of the Ornithopter. One of the closer insects had come within firing range and Brunois and Jahn both opened up. Hitting a flying target while flying themselves was a new experience for both of them. It almost reached them by the time they shot it enough to send it crashing to the ground below.

Another insect swooped upon them. The direct sunlight revealed it in all its horrific precision. The body was segmented into three sections and crowned by a glass-eyed head. Its wings were a blur of motion, and its six legs struck out, attempting to either latch onto or tear apart the Ornithopter's frame.

Auroka drew her bow and fired. Direct hit. The hideous creature plummeted from the sky amidst a crackling web of energy.

Two more chased the fleeing party. Everyone but Rana fired with all they had. The closer of the two jolted backward as the barrage of bullets bit into its metal body. A viscous fluid began to spurt from within. Its wings ceased to beat and down it went.

The second one swooped to the side and evaded Auroka's shimmering arrow. She fired another. It went wide.

Having exhausted the ammunition in their guns, Brunois and Jahn reloaded as quickly as their fingers could manage. The skin on their fingertips sung from the heat of the gunmetal.

Auroka drew her bow again and exhaled. The nocked arrow bristled with energy. She sighted her target and fired.

A bright light erupted from the center of the bug's abdomen. The winged creature fell away from them to the world below.

Brunois glanced over to the Peste. It had clamped itself firmly to his shoulder. He croaked out a chuckle. "Winds be too strong fer ya up 'ere then?"

A single blink.

Rana pitched the giant metal bird further forward and they made for Dunham on steam-powered wings.

CHAPTER

30

The sunset was beautiful. Reds, violets, oranges, and yellows cavorted around in a brilliant kaleidoscope. Light painted the clouds on the horizon, drawing them into its fiery dance.

Wourinos liked to watch the sunset. He stood on the wall by the East Gate and stared westward as it enveloped Dunham in its warm embrace. Red rooftops glowed, the stained-glass windows of the church sparkled, the citizens of the city scurried about, bathed in golden-red hues.

The inspector didn't like this whole Brunois and Rache business. Either of them alone was enough trouble, anything involving the both of them was certain to be twice as much, if not more. With any luck, neither of them would return to Dunham any time soon.

He turned around and looked out over the forested lands east of the city. Night was already taking a firm hold on them, the distant horizon now a deep purple as the last of the sun's rays withdrew from it. Wourinos swatted at a bug that buzzed around his face. He missed so he swatted again, but still, the bug evaded his hand.

Something in the distance caught his eye.

At first glance, it was just another bug come to harass him, but as the Badger fixed his gaze upon it, he realized it was something much larger and much farther off. It was traveling toward Dunham. Wourinos stared at it and attempted to discern its identity, and whether or not he should raise the alarm.

The growing shape took on a more definite form.

A bird? What bird is that big?

Massive wings flapped in a powerful rhythm. It came into the waning sun's reach and sparkled, the frame of its metal body becoming visible.

It's a machine!

Even more amazing were the forms of passengers within its belly. Wourinos realized he had become so enwrapped in the study of this thing that he had neglected to raise the alarm. He turned around and raised it. When he turned back, the flying machine was descending into a small clearing.

By the time he reached the bottom of the wall, a constable and two deputy constables had assembled. He nodded to them.

"You there, follow me. Weapons drawn and ready to fire." He waved his hand as he set out of the gate.

The others followed him into the woods, toward the clearing. At first, their pace was fast, but they slowed as they drew near due to the darkness, which was denser beneath the trees.

A loud crash echoed through the forest. Everyone went still for a moment. With nothing to observe from where they stood, Wourinos waved his party onward toward the noise.

The inspector and his constables slowly approached the grounded, mechanical, birdlike thing. There was movement from within it. Revolvers were raised and cocked.

"Who goes there?" Wourinos asked. "I am Inspector Wourinos of the Dunham Constabulary and I ask you to identify yourself."

"Wourinos! I am glad you are here." The voice was known to the Badger.

"Auroka?" His own voice was full of surprise. It was not like him to be surprised.

"I have a serious matter to report."

The Horse was a little banged up from their "landing," but nothing serious, and she quickly regained her hooves and strode over to Wourinos.

In the captain's chair of the beast, Rana was fumbling with her buckles. She managed to get them undone and staggered out onto the ground, falling to her hands and knees as she did.

Jahn disembarked and, after a moment to steady himself, joined Auroka.

Brunois unbuckled his straps and slipped out the other side of the Ornithopter and hid behind it.

"What news do you have to report?" Wourinos asked Auroka.

Her stare was heavy and haggard. "There is a swarm of metal insects headed this way. They have to be stopped. There is no telling how much damage they can do, no telling how many lives might be lost."

Auroka's words were pained, but whether from physical exhaustion or emotional terror Wourinos could not tell. Maybe it was both. She certainly looked as if it could be both.

The inspector nodded. "That is quite a story, Auroka. I'm not so sure I believe you. Where is it?"

Auroka's voice took on a commanding tone. "If it follows us, and it was, it will be here by morning. We must telegraph the Royal Army in Chevaire. Help must be sent."

A wary look swept across Wourinos. He glanced over the strange craft and its other passengers. There was a Mule who seemed the military sort, the red Frog pilot, who looked to be a young girl, and another figure that lurked on the far side of the contraption. He stared at the mystery figure, studying its silhouette and judging it to be another Frog. A Frog wearing a wide-brimmed hat and a sword strapped across its back. A brief flash of light on its shoulder revealed its face.

"Brunois!" the inspector called out. "Come around here and show yourself!"

The Peste earned a hard glare from Brunois for his untimely flicker and crawled inside the Frog's jacket. Brunois croaked out "Bleedin' metal bug…" as he walked around the body of the Ornithopter.

"Inspector, we haven't much time, we must send a message out now," Auroka pressed.

Wourinos looked over the group. "What's your stake in this, Brunois?" he asked.

Brunois slowly shook his head. "Nothin' now. We went lookin' fer something worthwhile in the ruins, but all we be findin' was that awful swarm o' mechanical bugs."

Wourinos was not convinced. "And Rache? What's his involvement?"

Another shake of the head from Brunois. This time with a grin. "Nothin' now. He followed us out there lookin' to kill us and take what we find. Instead, what we found killed all his pack."

"And you?" Wourinos asked, turning to face Jahn.

"Staff Sergeant Jahn Chomberdale, formerly of His Majesty's Army, at your service." Jahn stood at attention while speaking.

"Inspector, we do not have time for this, tell your men to lower their weapons and let's go into the city. You have a duty to the citizens." Auroka was adamant, summoning the full weight of her voice and stature as she spoke.

"Don't tell me about duty. You may be a Fiercheval, but you do not have the authority to order me to do anything, you who shunned your duties and responsibilities to go roam the wilds." Wourinos's voice rose. "And now you show up in this strange machine with a known criminal, claiming that a swarm of bugs is on its way to devour the city?"

Auroka looked the Badger square in the eye. "Why would I lie?"

Wourinos pursed his lips. "I've never heard of anything like that. I know there is a lot of Svargan technology out there that I've never seen, but that all sounds a bit much."

"Show him, Uncle Brunois," Rana said.

Brunois shook his jacket a little. A flickering light came flying out and hovered by his head. All guns immediately aimed at it.

"No!" Rana exclaimed as she jumped in front of the Peste. "He's not one of them. Well, he is a bug from there, but he's a good one. His name is the Peste."

It blinked a single time.

Everyone stared at the little brass firefly. It landed on Brunois's shoulder and stared back.

"Now do you believe me?" Auroka asked.

Wourinos took a moment to finish staring at the Peste but then said, "Yes, I suppose I do. Lower your weapons, lads, we're all going back to the headquarters. Tell me all about this while we walk."

CHAPTER

31

ORIG DUNHAM CONSTABULARY MSG BX45992 2031 HOURS

TO OFFICE OF DEFENSE MINISTER

AIRBORNE THREAT OF SVARGAN ORIGIN REPORTED—(STOP)—POSES IMMINENT DANGER TO DUNHAM AND ITS CITIZENS—(STOP)—ARRIVAL EXPECTED IN MORNING—(STOP)—SIZE OF FORCE IS UNKNOWN—(STOP)—SEND WHATEVER AID IS AVAILABLE—(STOP)—

INSPECTOR WOURINOS
DUNHAM CONSTABULARY

32

"You take the bed, Rana," Brunois said as he took a seat on the floor and leaned up against the wall.

Rana didn't argue. She hopped up on the single cot in the empty holding cell. It was rough and lumpy but a lot more comfortable than the cold, hard stone of the floor. A dampness clung to the gray stone walls, and the air smelled of something fermenting.

"You want the blanket?" she asked.

"Nah, I be fine." Brunois did his best to get comfortable. It wasn't going to happen. A jail cell was a jail cell, locked or not. The Peste sat on his shoulder, blinking every so often.

Wourinos had opened it up for them to get some rest in. It was only a moderately nice gesture since he also told them that they couldn't leave the constabulary headquarters until he gave his approval.

Rana settled into the cot. Her whole body ached with exhaustion. Even her bones hurt.

"Uncle Brunois?"

"Yeah?" he croaked out from under his hat, which he had tilted forward over his face.

"Thanks."

"Fer what?"

"For saving me."

"No need to be thankin' me."

"No. I do need to. You didn't have to let me come along, but you did. And when I got into trouble, you saved me. When I got lost, you came and looked for me. When I was captured, you rescued me."

"Ya be makin' me sound a lot nicer than I truly be. 'Sides, ya be savin' me too."

"Well…I guess that makes us even," she said in a playful voice.

Brunois croaked out a chuckle. "Get yerself some rest now, we be gettin' out o' here soon as Wourinos let us. Figure they no raised the alarm 'bout what Auroka said since it be pretty quiet in here, and I no hear nothin' out in th'streets either. Iffn' we can be outta here 'fore anyone be seein' the swarm, we can get a train to th'west er north."

A stillness hung between the stone walls of the cell.

"I'm not leaving," Rana said in a soft voice.

"What? What do ya mean ya not be leavin'?"

"I mean I'm going to stay and help fight."

"Have ya gone mad, Rana? What do ya think ya can do to fight them out in th'open? It was all we could do to be gettin' away from 'em when they were underground. Out 'ere, they be even more dangerous."

Rana sighed. "I know that. But I woke them. It's my responsibility to stay and fight them."

"It ain't yer fault they woke."

"Yes, it is. It was my fire that powered them all up."

"What? How? I no thought you were strong 'nough fer that…"

"Well, not directly. I started the machine that powered them all up, but that's the same thing. I can't leave everyone in this city without trying to fight."

"Ya don't be owin' th' folk o' this city nothin'. Most of 'em would leave you fer dead."

"I don't believe that. I believe there is good here."

Brunois croaked. "Ain't no good folk nowhere. I say we leave 'em all to they fate, whatever it might be."

Her voice was petulant. "Fine. Leave if you want, but I'm staying."

Brunois muttered something under his breath.

The two of them were still in the silence and darkness. None of the other cells around them held any prisoners. It was just them, the walls, and the bars.

The Peste stirred on Brunois's shoulder, taking off to hover in front of the Frog's face. It began to blink.

Brunois stared at it.

It stared back.

"What?" the Frog croaked at it. "Don't tell me ya think we should be stayin'?"

A single blink.

A croak. "Fool bug. Don't know nothin'."

They exchanged stares again for a while.

"Fine," Brunois finally said. "Guess I be stayin' too then."

"You will?"

"Yeah. Can't be lettin' ya get yerself killed. Never be able to face Arcator 'gain."

"Thanks, Uncle Brunois."

"I said no be callin' me uncle."

"I know."

Brunois took the winged key from his jacket and wound the Peste. Once done, the little brass firefly returned to its spot on the Frog's shoulder.

"Rana?"

"Yes?"

A long pause.

"Ya can call me uncle iffn' ya want."

"I know."

CHAPTER

33

Dawn brought many things to Dunham.

Auroka stood on the roof of the constabulary head-quarters and looked out over the city. The rising sun was waking up the sleeping populace, bringing with it a new day full of new possibilities. Down in the street below, she saw a young Fox walking with her Kit in tow, off to run a morning errand.

They don't even know what's coming.

She had managed to get Wourinos to telegraph the defense minister's office alerting them to the threat, but the obstinate Badger had refused to evacuate the city.

"A panic may kill more than this swarm would. I believe you saw something, but I won't start a panic based on a threat that I do not know is coming," he had told her.

She turned and faced westward. The towers of her family's home stuck out from what was known as the Silver Quarter. The term referred to all the coins that must be there. It was where the wealthy and the aristocracy resided. Her father, Duke Frederok Fiercheval, was probably still sleeping in his chambers there.

He must not know either. He'd have summoned me by now if he did.

Over the rooftops, the sky lightened by degrees. A black shape appeared within its violet expanse. It broke apart into three separate shapes as it journeyed toward the city, the one in the center being the largest. As the sunlight increased and the distance between Auroka and the three shapes decreased, she made out more of their forms. Each was mostly a large, red, oblong balloon with a much smaller structure suspended below.

Only three?

They reached the West Gate of the city and slowed to drop anchor. She went below to alert Wourinos of the airships' arrival.

"They are at the West Gate. Let's gather Brunois and Rana and go meet them," she told the inspector.

Wourinos frowned. "I don't want to bring them with us. It is not a matter for civilians. Especially not Brunois."

"They have firsthand knowledge of what we face. The commander of the airships might have questions they are able to answer," she said back.

Jahn spoke up from where he sat by the wall in Wourinos's office. "I agree. They've fought these things before. If they are willing to come, they will be a help."

Wourinos nodded. "Fine then, but it's on you."

Brunois and Rana were up and ready to go when they arrived at the holding cells. The five of them, and the Peste, headed out. The halls of the constabulary headquarters were relatively quiet, given the hour, and the group quickly made their way from the stone walls of the holding cells to the wood-paneled ones of the office. Once out on the equally quiet streets, they set off for the West Gate. The sound of their feet and hooves on the cobblestones echoed off of the brick buildings common to that quarter of the city.

"Only three airships? That no gonna be enough fer what's comin' 'ere," Brunois croaked.

"It will have to be," Auroka said back.

Brunois grumbled.

The Peste landed on his shoulder and blinked a few times.

Halfway to the gate, they were met by a constable, a well-groomed Dog in a freshly laundered uniform. He hailed Wourinos. "Inspector Wourinos! It is good to see you, sir. I was just coming to fetch you. A group of airships has arrived, and their captain has asked to speak with you personally."

"Yes, I know. We saw them arrive and are on our way," Wourinos replied.

The constable eyed the rest of the party but said nothing further, merely turned, and walked with them.

At the West Gate, they were greeted by a tall, slender Fox with red fur. He was dressed in a brown leather jacket, trousers, and boots, all of which were lined with extra padding. Golden captain's bars were on his epaulets.

"Ho there!" he called out to the approaching party. "Captain Mourgan, at your service. I'm looking for Inspector Wourinos."

The inspector stepped forth and offered his hand, which the captain took and shook briskly.

"This is some of my squadron, the Flying Foxes of His Majesty's Royal Air Corps." He waved his hand back to a few other Foxes dressed in similar fashion, who stood nearby. "Now then, why don't you tell me just what it is we're doing out here?"

Auroka stepped forward. "I should probably answer that."

"And who might you be?" Captain Mourgan asked.

"This is Lady Auroka Fiercheval, Captain," Wourinos answered. "She is the one who alerted me to this potential threat."

"All right then, Lady Fiercheval," the captain said coolly, "what is going on out here?"

"A little over two days ago, Brunois, Rana, and I"—she nodded toward the Frogs—"entered an underground Svargan ruin east of here. We had been followed by a criminal pack led by a Dog named Rache and were attacked by them. During the battle, we stumbled upon what I can only describe as a massive mechanical hive. Something woke it up, and we fled. The flying swarm followed us, but we were able to outrun it and make it here."

The captain nodded. "And where is it now?"

"I don't know."

"How were you able to outrun it if it's flying?"

"We were able to use an old, experimental flying machine."

The captain chuckled. "Some story. But I came all the way down here, might as well go take a look so I have something to report on."

"We should come with you," Auroka said. "We can help."

The captain shook his head. "Out of the question, miss. I don't just bring civilians along on a reconnaissance mission. But maybe when we're done, I'll take you up for ride?" He winked at her.

"That's ridiculous!" Rana blurted out. "You're going to need us!"

Captain Mourgan laughed. It was a hearty bellow. "And what makes you think that, girlie?"

"We've fought these things already," Rana answered.

"And ran from them," he said back.

Rana bristled. "You have to let us come."

The captain shook his head again. "No, that's not going to happen." He turned to Wourinos and asked, "Anything you want to add, Inspector?"

Wourinos shook his head.

"All right then. I'll report what I find." He turned and walked back to the rope ladder dangling from the largest of the three airships. "All right, lads, up anchor and set our heading due east!"

Rana turned to Auroka. Their stares were equally angry.

"What do we do now?" Rana asked.

The Peste began to blink furiously and took off from Brunois's shoulder. Everyone turned to look at it as it ascended, facing eastward.

"Think you can get the Ornithopter back in the air, Rana?" Auroka asked.

Rana just nodded and stared out at the eastern horizon. A low-lying gray cloud was growing on it. She would get her chance to help after all. The swarm was coming to Dunham.

CHAPTER

34

Brunois checked his weapons as they came to the East Gate. It had taken them over an hour to get there. They had first gone back to the constabulary headquarters so Wourinos could raise the alarm. From there, one of the constables took them in a horse-drawn carriage the rest of the way across the city. Now they were off to where Rana had set the Ornithopter down.

Auroka led the way, with Jahn right behind her. The two Frogs managed to keep up with the Peste flying alongside them. The Ornithopter was where they had left it, and they all hopped aboard and buckled them-selves in.

Wourinos had initially protested their plan but in the end agreed with the logic of it and had allowed them to take whatever they wanted from the armory before departing. Brunois and Jahn had both taken high-caliber rifles and plenty of ammunition. They had each taken a pair of tinted goggles, which they slipped over their heads as Rana settled into the captain's chair.

She closed her eyes and began to fuel the fire in her mind. At the rear of the flying machine, the boiler shuddered to life as the water heated up. The wings began to beat, slowly at first, but they picked up speed as Rana continued to focus. Her emotions ran high—anger, determination, fear and excitement; she channeled them all into heating that boiler. The wings flapped fast enough to lift them from the ground, and off they went toward the Flying Foxes and the swarm.

In the back, Brunois, Auroka, and Jahn were tying ropes around their bodies and securing them to the frame. Once done, they unbuckled themselves from the benches and selected firing positions. Auroka took the tail while the other two took the starboard and port sides of the Ornithopter.

The Peste crawled inside Brunois's jacket and stayed there, not being able to withstand the higher altitude winds as the party soared through them on steampowered wings. Below, the trees and grasses of the forest blurred into amorphous green shapes, idyllic in the golden light of the now risen sun. The black blotch of the swarm grew and cast its shadow at their approach.

"Were coming up on them!" Rana called out.

Up ahead, the three airships slowly moved northward in a single line. The massive propellers on their sterns, with blades the size of a windmill's, powered them forward. From their starboard sides, they were firing into the swarm. Metal shapes churned and writhed against each other as the scattershot fire from the ships' guns tore into them.

Rana banked to the left and then back to the right, attempting to flank the swarm and stay out of the Flying Foxes' field of fire. They would have to get closer than the other airships to be effective, so to be safe, she pitched the Ornithopter back and took to a higher altitude. Cries of surprise came from behind her.

"Give us a bit o' warnin' iffn' yer gonna be doin' that, Rana!" Brunois exclaimed. "We coulda fallen out!"

He didn't have much time to protest, though. The swarm was rapidly coming into range.

Shimmering arrows began to slice through the sky as Auroka shot into the cloud of metal shapes. Each hit was marked by a brief flash and followed by ripples of energy diffusing outward over some of the other mechanical insects.

Brunois knelt down and hooked his leg around one of the benches in the Ornithopter's belly. He began to sight targets and fire, using the rifle's lever action to reload the chamber after each shot. Beside him, Jahn did the same with the practiced movements of a soldier.

Metal bugs fell from the sky. Rana banked left and flew back in the other direction. The shooters in the back switched to the other side and opened fire. Some targets they hit. Others they didn't.

It didn't seem to matter. For every one of the things they sent to the ground, two more took its place from the heart of the mechanical gyre. And now they were coming after the Ornithopter. Dozens of them broke away from the swarm and flew toward the flying machine.

Rana banked again and took off back toward the airships. Everyone in the back continued to fire. Light pierced the air as Auroka let arrow after arrow fly, waves of energy crackling in their wakes. But the insects were gaining.

A few hundred feet below them, the airship squadron was not faring any better. The swarm continued to press toward them. Each roar of the deck guns sent several of the flying abominations hurtling earthward, but it just wasn't enough. There were too many of them. The lead ship, the largest of the three, accelerated and began to pull away. The next ship in line followed suit. The third was not fast enough.

Brunois looked down and saw the insects land on the deck. He couldn't hear the screams of the men, but knew they were there. The swarm began to envelop the whole of the ship. Wood and metal broke away from the hull and fell from the sky. In a matter of minutes, it was nothing but debris on the ground below.

"Brunois!" Auroka called. "Keep firing!"

Brunois looked up to see several insects closing in on them from behind. He raised his rifle and began shooting.

Auroka fired as fast as she could. Her arms, shoulders, and back ached from continually drawing her bow. Her mind felt drained from the exertion of conjuring the arrows. But she kept firing, and the bugs kept falling.

Jahn stopped to reload. That was all it took. One of the insects swooped down below the Ornithopter and then rapidly ascended on it. A metal leg speared him through the torso. He couldn't even manage a scream.

The insect clamped onto the frame of the Ornithopter. Its extra weight caused the flying machine to roll. Brunois was thrown off his feet, falling through the belly of it and out the other side. The world spun in a dizzying swirl of vertigo. Wind whipped past his head in cold slices as he plummeted into the sky. It was only the rope wound around his waist that prevented him from making the trip all the way to the forest floor.

Auroka managed to keep her hooves and turned to see her friend struggling against his impaler.

"Jahn!" she screamed and drew her bow.

The insect looked up at her. She was standing so close to it she could see the reflection of her arrow in its amber glass eyes. She fired.

At that range, its head exploded from the force, and the horrid thing toppled backward, releasing its grip on the Ornithopter's frame. Jahn, however, was not gripped, but skewered, and went with it. The extra weight of the bug caused the rope to snap when it reached its end, and the bug and the Mule tumbled out of the sky to the world below.

Brunois watched in horror as the dual form of Jahn and insect fell past him. The Mule was still alive and looked Brunois in the eye. Jahn's expression was proud. He was dying a soldier's death, an honorable death.

With the extra weight gone from the side of the Ornithopter, Rana was able to level the craft back out. Brunois trailed behind it, swinging from the rope. He tossed his rifle away so he would have both hands to climb with and began to pull himself back toward the Ornithopter. Above his head, Auroka continued to fire.

By the time Brunois reached the rear of the flying machine, Auroka was there to offer a hand and help him back on board. She handed him Jahn's rifle without saying a word.

Brunois took up a firing position and resumed shooting at the swarm.

The two airships below were retreating. Rana dipped the nose of her aircraft forward and descended to aid the smaller of them, which was bringing up the rear. Her heart was beating out of her chest. Adrenaline flooded her system. The boiler churned and shook with the force of her emotions being funneled into it as searing heat.

Flying constructs were all around. The Foxes on the deck continued to fire into the swarm, but they just couldn't keep up with the press of them. Bugs began to land on the deck and tear into the crewmen. Auroka and Brunois did their best to shoot at the assailing force of metal limbs and shiny wings. It was not enough.

The swarm overtook the second airship, tearing it asunder. Beams and planks, hull and device alike were rent from one another by the clawing metal monstrosities. One of the Foxes jumped off the side railing. After a few moments, a parachute opened behind him. It was a beacon to the swarm, which quickly descended upon the poor soul.

Rana was forced to bank away. Tears were forming at the corners of her eyes—tears of anger, tears of despair. She was angry at the loss of life. She despaired there was nothing she could do about it. Each new wave of emotion was converted into fire and applied to the boiler.

The largest, and only remaining, airship set a westward course back toward Dunham. Rana flew up alongside of it, close enough that they could make out one another's figures, if not determine exactly who was on the deck.

Both crafts gave it everything they had in their effort to outrun the swarm. It was sufficient to get them back to Dunham ahead of the impending doom.

35

Rana's second attempt at landing the Ornithopter was much better than the first, which had been more of a crash. The party disembarked by the East Gate, one member notably absent.

Nearby, the remaining airship's anchor fell to the ground, followed by a rope ladder, and then Captain Mourgan. The Fox was ashen-faced as he walked over to meet Rana, Auroka, Brunois, and the Peste.

"We need to get word back to Chevaire," he said. "The rest of the Royal Air Corps needs to be sent."

Auroka nodded. "How long will they take to arrive?"

"I can't say for certain. There was only one other squadron docked when I left the aerodrome. Hopefully the others will be reachable."

"Well, let's not be wastin' time 'ere then runnin' our mouths," Brunois croaked out and set off for the East Gate.

Constables were stationed on the walls of the city, setting up mounted guns in preparation for defense. Inside the walls, the streets teemed with Dunham's citizens, all trying to flee or find safe haven.

Brunois led the way as best he could. There was a telegraph office close by, if they could just manage to push through the mob in the streets. Panic reigned, and they all got jostled about as they attempted to maneuver down the street.

"What news of the swarm?" a voice called out.

Brunois turned to see Wourinos standing by the doorway to a church. He led the others over.

Captain Mourgan spoke up first. "Two of my ships are down, along with the twenty-four men who flew them. The swarm is still coming. I estimate it will arrive here in less than three hours. I need to get a message to Chevaire."

"I be tryin' to get 'em to the telegraph office, two blocks over," Brunois said.

Wourinos nodded and waved over two of his deputies. "Escort Captain Mourgan to the telegraph office on Walnut Street."

The two deputy constables nodded and left with Captain Mourgan behind them.

"How much of the city has been evacuated?" Auroka asked the inspector.

Wourinos sighed. "None. Some are fleeing, but given how quickly the swarm would be here, the chief constable thought it best to bring as many as possible inside easily defensible positions. I've been assigned to the cathedral here."

"What are we going to do?" Rana asked. Her voice was raw with fear and doubt.

Wourinos slowly shook his head. "Dig in and try and hold them until the rest of the Royal Air Corps can be dispatched, and pray they are able to destroy the threat."

Rana went wide-eyed. "But by then, the swarm will be on top of the city! Everyone will die by the time they get here!"

"Quiet down, girl!" Wourinos said to her. "Everyone is already panicked enough, let's not add to it. Come inside and we can talk someplace quiet."

The group went inside and began walking toward the altar. The walls were lined with statues and stained-glass windows, although the windows were now obscured by barricades. The Peste earned many stares from those inside. With the swarm pending, a mechanical bug was not met with much trust.

At the altar, they gathered in a circle.

"We have to hold off the swarm, keep them from reaching the city as long as possible," Auroka said. "What are our options?"

Silence.

"I no think there be anythin' we can be doin'. Flyin' back out there be suicide and won't even slow 'em down more than a few minutes at best," Brunois finally croaked out.

They all stared at one another.

"Well, what do we do then?" Rana asked in a defeated voice.

"We pray," Wourinos said.

"Pray?" The question was asked by Rana, Brunois, and Auroka all at once. The Peste blinked a few times.

Wourinos nodded. "Pray."

"I ain't 'xactly the prayin' sort, mate," Brunois said.

"Will you pray with me now?" Wourinos asked him.

The Frog thought about it a moment. "Aye, I suppose I will then."

There, below a statue of Eshua, the Great Lion, they joined hands. Wourinos led the prayer.

"Lord Eshua, you gave your life for us all those hundreds of years ago. You did it so we could have a chance at a new life, so we could live a life free from all the horrors of the past. Now those horrors attack us again. Please, come to us in our time of need. We believe you are still with us, and that you still love us. We need your power desperately, show us the way. Adgratum."

"Adgratum," they replied in unison, even Brunois. The Peste blinked a single time.

Everyone opened their eyes and looked at one another.

They waited.

"I no feel any different," Brunois said.

A bustle of bodies came up from the back.

"I have good news!" Captain Mourgan called out to them as he approached with the two deputy constables. "I got word to the admiral. Much of the fleet has just returned from the north. They can be here within six hours."

"How many airships is that?" Auroka asked him.

"Six class A warships, plus ten class B destroyers, and another twenty class C skirmishers. My vessel, the Dove, is a class B destroyer." He grinned a little. "Looks like we have some hope."

"Iffn' we all live that long. That swarm is gonna get 'ere first. I no doubt it can kill half o' th' city 'fore the fleet even be gettin' ere," Brunois croaked.

"And then the battle will be over top of the city," Rana said. "We have to find a way to stall them, and I think I have one."

All eyes were on Rana.

"Tell me, Captain," she said, "what's in that balloon that keeps your airship afloat?"

Captain Mourgan gave her a hard look but then broke into a laugh. "Ha! That just might work, missy! If we can get far enough into the swarm that is. How do you plan to detonate it, though? It will take a strong flame to spark it."

Rana smiled and held out her hand. A small flame appeared in it and then rapidly shot up into blazing column of fire.

Captain Mourgan blinked. "Yes. That should do, I think."

Rana looked over to Wourinos. "Do you have dynamite in the armory?"

Wourinos nodded and called the two deputy constables back over. "Go to the armory and bring back as much dynamite as you can carry, on the double quick."

"If yer sayin' what I think ya be sayin', Rana, I no like this plan one bit," Brunois muttered.

Rana grinned. "I know."

36

Brunois fed shells into the breech of his rifle while the crew of the Dove loaded the crates of dynamite on board. He liked this rifle and hoped that he would be able to keep it after this was over.

If I survive.

The Peste blinked a few times and looked Brunois in the eye from where it sat on the Frog's shoulder.

Brunois returned the wary stare and croaked out, "Me too. Me too."

The Ornithopter, in which he sat, had already been loaded onto the deck using a series of pulleys and winches that the airship was outfitted with. That had been fortunate, because without them, this whole plan would have been a suicide mission. Now, it was just one with a very slim chance of survival.

"Hurry up, lads! We need to be underway in the next ten minutes! Get that cargo secured to the deck and man your stations!" Captain Mourgan strode down the starboard side of his airship, every inch the officer such a command required.

The crew of the Dove moved in frantic exertion, hurrying to finish the final preparations. Auroka stood at the bow of the vessel, staring out at the swarm, which was no more than a few miles off from the city. The midday sun shone bright from the cloudless sky. Sunlight rippled through her coppery ringlets as they swayed in the slight breeze, making them as tendrils of fire cascading down her back.

Rana was at the back of the Ornithopter, checking over the boiler and other apparatuses. She had gotten a wrench from a stout Fox, who was the Dove's mechanic, and was tightening down some bolts and fittings. It all came quite naturally to her, surprisingly so, in fact. Rana herself was amazed at how easily she made sense of the different pipes, tubes, and cylinders.

"Ya sure ya want to be goin' through with this, Rana?" Brunois asked his niece as he walked around to her.

The wrench went still in her hand. She closed her eyes a moment and then stared into her uncle's eyes. "Yes. I have to."

"And you still no think we can't just be usin' a fuse fer the dynamite?"

"It's too risky. We don't know if the bugs will destroy the fuse or the dynamite. If we want this to work, this is the only way."

Brunois nodded. "All right then. I be with ya the whole way." He laid a reassuring hand on her shoulder. It communicated something to her that his words had never expressed.

She was grateful for it.

Captain Mourgan gathered his crew on the port side of the deck.

"All right then, it has been an honor to serve with you all. You are a credit to His Majesty's Royal Air Corps, and there is no finer squadron than the Flying Foxes. I personally selected each one of you for your bravery and loyalty. Now I ask you to disembark the Dove. In order for this mission to be a success, we need to be flying as light as possible, and we will only be able to provide a means of egress for a few. If I do not make it back, know that I hold all of you in highest regard."

He stood at attention and saluted his men. They were apprehensive, but they saluted back and barked out, "Aye-aye, Captain." Then, one at a time, they went down the rope ladder.

Captain Mourgan turned to those that remained: Auroka, Rana, Brunois, and The Peste. "Time to go?"

They all nodded.

The captain took his saber and cut the rope holding the anchor. "I don't think we shall need that again."

The Dove began to rise into the sky. Its captain stood at the wheel and pointed the bow straight at the oncoming mass of mechanical death.

Without the extra weight, the airship picked up speed quickly and was soon traveling well over seventy knots. The wind on the deck was fierce, and the Peste sought refuge inside of Brunois's jacket. He was comforted by the Peste's presence, a fact he would never admit to anyone though. He took up a firing position toward the bow on the port side, opposite Auroka.

Brunois unslung his rifle. Auroka unslung her bow. Up ahead, the swarm took on more definition as they approached it. The individual insects became distinguishable, writhing and gyrating against one another as they approached Dunham.

Rana took one final look over the Ornithopter and then headed to the bow to join her uncle. She was already feeling the rush of adrenaline in her limbs. Her hands were warm. It took little effort to conjure fireballs in them.

"Hold on!" Captain Mourgan called out. His voice sounded distant and hollow.

Brunois heard his heartbeat ringing in his ears. The sheer stress of their situation heightened his senses. The cool air that whipped by his face was sweet with oil and grease. The bright sun overhead reflected millions of sparkles within the churning mass of metal limbs, into which they now plunged.

Beside him, a shimmering beacon of light caught the corner of his eye as Auroka drew her bow. He turned to look at her; she was calm and focused as she loosed the arrow.

Over a hundred feet off the bow, one of the swarm contracted in a spasm of light and plummeted groundward.

Brunois opened fire. He barely took time to aim at each target. They had elected not to use the ship's deck guns since no one but Captain Mourgan was skilled in the operation of them, and without them, they were that much lighter.

And I do like this rifle.

They drew closer to the swarm, firing into it with everything they could muster.

Rana threw searing balls of fire. Explosions littered the mass of insects as she tossed her flames into it. She did her best to keep the assault constant, but it was taxing on her already exhausted body, and there was a lot more to be done yet.

The deck of the Dove lurched from side to side as Captain Mourgan began to steer the airship back and forth. His hope was that by keeping steady lateral motion, they could brush off some of the would-be attackers and prevent them from landing on the deck or the envelope above it. There would be no turning around and firing from the three up on the bow, so he had to do his best to keep the airship free of the giant bugs.

All around them, the swarm churned with excitement and directed its ire on the airship. Brunois turned to face port, Auroka starboard, and the pair continued to fire as fast as they could. Both had eschewed accuracy in favor of volume. With the number of targets that now assailed the Dove, it was nigh impossible to *not* hit one of the insects when they shot.

Still facing forward into the swarm, Rana took a deep breath and channeled all the anger, rage, frustration, and passion she had in her. She threw her hands out, and a cone of flame erupted forth. Red and orange tore through the sea of metal. It was blindingly bright and blazingly hot. Insects fell from the sky in droves, their charred bodies smashing into their brethren below as they toppled downward.

Brunois continued to fire as he backed toward the Ornithopter. He wore an ammunition belt across his chest to make reloading the rifle faster. It was a wise choice. Some of the insects had begun to land on the railing of the Dove. Brunois could dispense them with two rifle shots if they were well placed. More if they were not.

He reached the Ornithopter and grabbed one of the ropes they had attached earlier. Auroka had already arrived and clipped one on to her belt. They both continued to fire, doing their best to keep the deck free of assailants.

"Rana!" Brunois called out. "Get yerself back 'ere! This be it!"

Up above at the helm, Captain Mourgan took a metal bar and slid it through the spokes of the wheel, locking it in place. He gave the housing a final pat and said, "Good-bye, old girl," then jumped over the railing and ran toward the Ornithopter.

Once there, he slid into the captain's chair and strapped in. Rana had asked him earlier if he would be able to fly it. "Missy, I can fly anything" had been his reply. He hoped he was right.

The cone of flame springing from Rana's hands dissipated. The roar of the fire still echoed in her ears. She fell to one knee.

"Rana!" Brunois yelled out again.

She didn't move.

An insect landed on the prow of the airship. Sharp and shiny appendages sunk into the wood. It eyed Rana and raised its forelegs. They descended toward Rana's tiny Frog body.

Bullets chewed into the insect from further aft on the ship's deck. Brunois charged forward, revolvers out. He emptied both of them.

The bug jerked and jittered backward. With a final pop, its eyes went dark and it toppled headlong into the sky.

Rana looked up from where she crouched. She summoned what little energy she had left and gained her feet, taking Brunois's arm as he came beside her. The pair of Frogs hobbled back to the Ornithopter and clipped themselves in, grateful for Auroka's covering fire.

"Let's get out of here!" Captain Mourgan called back to them.

Rana closed her eyes and exhaled slowly. The Ornithopter's boiler clanked and shuddered to life. She poured her whole soul into it.

On either side of her, Brunois and Auroka continued to fire. The insects were now tearing apart the deck of the ship and entering the cabins below. It would not remain airborne much longer. Any insect that encroached upon the Ornithopter was met with bullets or blazing arrows of light. Sometimes both.

"Rana!" Brunois called out. "We need to be gettin' out o' here! Now!"

The little Frog clenched her jaw and squeezed her little Froggy spirit. The wings began to beat.

37

The Ornithopter left the wooden deck of the Dove behind. Not much of the airship was still distinguishable beneath the teeming sprawl of metal limbs and pincers, all gnashing and tearing at the aerostatic vessel. Chunks of wood and metal came away in scores as the swarm chewed through the Dove's hull.

Captain Mourgan would have sighed at the sight if he wasn't so busy staying alive. He banked and swooped to evade the flying mechanical insects. From within the heart of the swarm, it was no easy feat to accomplish. Bullets and brilliant arrows flew as Brunois and Auroka shot into the mass of metal bugs.

"Ya might want to start workin' on th'Dove!" Brunois yelled to his niece as he cocked the lever action on his rifle and shot a wasp-like automaton at point blank range. The thing's head exploded in a shower of metal slivers and shards of glass.

Rana stared at the envelope of the Dove. "I need to wait until we get a little further," she yelled back. "I won't be able to focus on that and our boiler here at the same time, so we might go into free fall once I start!"

"Well, that's just wonderful!" Captain Mourgan's voice was difficult to make out over the howl of the wind and the hum of the swarm. With every dip and roll of the Ornithopter, the other passengers had to hold fast to whatever was closest as the world spun and turned.

Auroka kept her leg firmly clamped around a piece of the flying machine's frame and did her best to keep shooting. There were just so many of them. A pair of pincers snapped at her hooves from below. She buried a shimmering arrow in them.

Rana could wait no longer, for fear they would travel beyond the range she could detonate the gas that kept the Dove aloft. "I'm gonna do it now!" She stared hard at the airship and focused her every fiber on it.

The Ornithopter's wings began to slow their pace. "Hold on!" Captain Mourgan hollered as he pulled back on the stick and tried to keep the nose up. Gunfire and shining arrows continued to pour out of the sides and back of the aircraft. The flying insects continued to swirl and gyrate around, seeking to rend the Ornithopter asunder. Its speed slowed. Its altitude diminished.

At the back, Rana continued to poured her little Froggy heart into igniting the envelope of the Dove. She reached deep into her soul, scrambling and scraping for whatever strength she had left. Her spirit wrung itself in agony, straining to give just a little more. In her mind's eye, she saw the fire forming. She could feel its heat inside her—small, but growing. With each breath, she stoked the furnace. Her whole body shook under the stress. Her vision went fuzzy. Her ears were filled with nothing but a great whoosh. She tuned out everything around her. The flame became her whole existence.

The blast was enormous.

The flash of light came first, followed shortly thereafter by a roaring boom. Reds, oranges, yellows, blacks, and grays churned over each other as the great airship combusted. It looked alive. A rapidly expanding organism that consumed all it came into contact with, swallowing insects within its waxing form.

A second flash came. The dynamite. It was not as large as the first, but the already swelling form of rolling flame lurched with sudden growth.

The wall of heat hit the Ornithopter, bringing with it blown apart bits of the metal bugs. The flying machine pitched and rolled. Its wings shot up to their topmost range of movement. One of them snapped part way off.

Brunois clenched his jaw as the horizon spun round at a dizzying rate. His stomach alternated between occupying his head and his feet. The part of the craft's frame that he clung to was all he could focus on. Time stretched out into eternity as their plummeting began to feel infinite. The world had disappeared, leaving only a great, yawning pit that let out into a void of emptiness.

Just get m'through this. Please. He didn't think the words so much as feel them. The primal fear that welled up within him overrode all else.

There was a sudden jarring impact, then blackness.

CHAPTER

38

Brunois was lost. He was surrounded by a thick fog that curled and undulated around him. There was nothing to be seen but the billowing grayness of it. No sky. No ground. No horizon. Just infinite, monochromatic formlessness.

A flicker of light flashed briefly.

What was that?

He tried to walk toward it, but he could not feel his legs. He couldn't feel any of his body. It was as if it wasn't there.

What be goin' on? Where am I?

Flicker.

He strained to see the source of the light but could discern nothing. The expanse of gray fog stretched out into eternity all around him. Strange sounds rang in his ears, distant and muffled.

Flicker.

Determined to discover what it was, he willed himself to move toward it. The surrounding grayness swirled and parted. He moved a tiny bit.

Flicker.

Brunois pushed harder, summoning as much willpower as he could to propel himself toward the light. He had no idea what it was, but it was the only thing different in the unending swirl of fog around him, so he went to it. His speed increased, the billowing plumes around him began to stretch and thin. A sensation like coming up from underwater washed over him.

The light flickered intensely.

He opened his eyes and inhaled sharply. The Peste was all he could see, staring him in the face and blinking rapidly. Brunois exhaled and let his head drop back to the ground.

The world around gradually appeared to him. Smoke curled upward from tangled metal piles. The air was acrid with smoldering sweetness. Naked trees were all around, stripped of branch and leaf by the debris as it fell from the sky. A few small fires ate through dry patches of vegetation, crackling amid twitching mechanical limbs that convulsed and rattled with death throes.

Brunois regained his feet and looked around for anyone else. Beyond a ridge of churned soil, he saw Auroka standing up, her fiery hair dulled with mud and singed by flame. She met his stare and the two began to walk toward one another.

"Ya be all right?" Brunois called out.

"I think so." She walked with a slight limp and held her left shoulder, but she didn't seem to be bleeding from anything but a few scrapes.

A sharp pain stabbed Brunois in his side with each step. It took the wind out of him. *Probably broke a rib or two.*

Off to his left, Captain Mourgan was crouched on a knee, holding a hand to his face. His leather uniform was torn and burned, as was much of the fur beneath it. He didn't notice Brunois and Auroka's approach.

"Mourgan! Ya be all right?"

The captain looked up at Brunois. The left side of his face was badly burned, and when he let his hand fall from it, a deep gash was visible. It ran from the top of his forehead and down the left side of his muzzle. The eye was gone. "I think I'll live."

Up above, what remained of the swarm writhed in on itself. Much of it had been destroyed in the blast, and many more still fell from the sky as their mangled forms gave out.

It worked. Just hope it be enough.

"Anyone see Rana?" Brunois asked.

Captain Mourgan shook his head and clutched his face again. "I'm not seeing much of anything."

Auroka turned and walked off to search. "No. But we'll find her."

Panic didn't grip Brunois's heart until their search bore no fruit after several minutes. They sorted through the heaps of wreckage and upturned forest. Fresh trenches had been carved into the soil by plummeting metal. Trees had been knocked over as broken machines toppled into them. Rocks had been split and charred. But no sign of Rana.

The Peste kept close to Brunois as he searched. With each new location, it flew around to illuminate whatever may be there. Every sigh from the Frog was met with a few flickers of sympathy from the Peste.

"Rana!" he called out, hoping for a response, but none came. His spirit sank, and panic set in.

"Rana!"

Silence.

The sensation in his heart was awful. It felt like his very soul was withering inside him. Nothing had ever felt this bad. He deflated onto his knees in despair.

"I'm sorry, Rana. I'm so sorry."

All of a sudden, the Peste took off into the brush, blinking excitedly. Brunois hopped to his feet and bounded after it, ignoring the stabbing pain in his side. He followed the flickering light, navigating between rocks and wreckage until they came to a streambed. Rana's body lay in it.

"Rana!"

He leapt down to her side and grabbed her by the arms, shaking her a bit, trying to wake her. "Rana! Wake up!"

Nothing.

"Rana! I need ya to be wakin' up now. Don't ya dare be dyin' on me. Not after all this. Not after all this." Tears were streaming from his eyes, running down the sides of his face. The Peste stayed by his shoulder and remained dark.

"Rana…" He gently let her limp body back down to the ground and hunched over her.

Pray.

He wasn't sure if that thought was his own. It sounded more like someone else's voice inside his head. No, not his head. His heart.

Pray for her.

He stammered and choked on his sorrow as he searched for words. All that came from his mouth were strained, noiseless wails of agony. Shallow breaths punctuated his wordless monologue in staccato fashion.

Pray for her.

He managed to level out his breathing and open his eyes.

"Iffn' ya can hear me… Iffn' yer there… please, save her. She be worth it. She be good. Please, she no deserve to die like this. Iffn' ya want someone, take me. But please, God, or whoever ya be, please be savin' her life. Just let her breathe 'gain. She be too young to be dyin' like this…"

The sorrow overtook him again, and his speech turned back to choking sobs. The Peste landed on his shoulder. It was all it could do.

Auroka and Mourgan stood on the bank of the stream, looking down on the Frogs. Their hearts broke for both of them.

Up above, the clouds moved away from the sun, and light streamed down through the broken and charred forest canopy. The golden rays swept over the Frogs, the younger one still held fast by the older. The sunlight's touch was warm and peaceful.

Rana's eyes fluttered open.

"Rana!" Brunois stared into her red face, hope soaring in his heart. "Rana! Are ya all right?"

She coughed, wheezed, and winced, but then she laid her head back on the ground and looked at her uncle. "Did it work?"

Brunois croaked out a small chuckle. "Aye. It worked."

The Peste blinked a single time. And then a whole bunch of times in a very ecstatic manner.

The roar of large guns drifted down to the huddled Frogs. They looked up to see a fleet of wood and steel flying into view. It was firing on the swarm, blasting what remained of it from the sky. It had worked indeed.

CHAPTER

39

Rana had never slept so well in her life. She had also never been so tired in all of her life. Silken quilts and goose-down pillows helped too. They helped a lot. She had spent the whole first day in bed and the better part of the second morning. Reluctant though she was, she eventually got up.

Her clothes had been laundered, although new ones had been laid out for her. She slipped into the pretty blue dress and white shoes and then twirled a few times in front of the mirror.

Maybe I'll wear them just for a little bit. You don't want to seem ungrateful.

Outside of her bedroom door was the rest of the Fierchevals' Dunham estate. Rana walked down the hallway, taking the time to admire all the things she had paid no mind to earlier. They had received a hero's welcome when they arrived back in Dunham. The whole city had turned out to celebrate her, Brunois, Auroka, and Captain Mourgan, as well as the rest of the fleet that had arrived. Frederok Fiercheval himself, Duke of Dunham, had been there to extend the thanks of the city and the hospitality of his own home. No one argued.

The house itself was massive and old. Thick carpeting was laid over a stone floor, and the woodworking along the banisters and wainscoting was exquisite. All around were paintings, statues, and other trappings of culture and aristocracy. The hallway that Rana walked down was easily a hundred feet long and was in what was regarded as the "small" wing of the home.

As she rounded a corner and descended the stairs into the foyer, she saw a few familiar figures. Her pace quickened, but she was forced to slow back down because of the cute, white shoes she was wearing. "Captain Mourgan! Inspector Wourinos!"

At the base of the staircase stood the Fox and the Badger, along with Auroka, Brunois, and the Peste. The five of them all turned at Rana's exclamation and laughed a little as she stumbled while trying to run in her new shoes.

"Ya look quite pretty there, Rana." Her uncle smiled at her and gave her a hug. "Finally up, eh?"

Rana giggled and looked around at the group. "Well, I just had to have something to eat."

Captain Mourgan saluted the little Frog as she walked up on the group. The left side of his face was wrapped in white cloth, covering where his eye had once been. "It is good to see you again, Ms. Rana."

"Thank you, Captain Mourgan." She did a mock curtsy.

The Fox laughed. "I wanted to call on you here before I returned to Chevaire with the rest of the fleet. You are recovering well from your exertions, I hope?"

"Why, thank you, captain. And yes, yes, I am."

Captain Mourgan nodded and smiled at her. "Well then, I also wish to inform you that for services rendered, the Crown would like to grant you a favor. Do you have anything in mind?"

Rana pursed her lips and thought on the question.

"You do not have to decide now, if you do not wish to. I understand it is a bit much to choose so suddenly."

"No, I think I shall choose. I would like to be able to study at the Royal Academy," she said with a definitive nod.

"A wise choice, miss. Your uncle merely asked for gold." He winked at Brunois.

"Hey, what be wrong with gold?" Brunois croaked at Captain Mourgan.

"Nothing, old chap. Nothing at all. Now if you'll excuse me, I'm expected on board in the next twenty minutes. I'll see to it you have your accommodations at the academy secured, Rana, and the Crown thanks you again." He gave a bow to all in the room, seizing the opportunity to kiss Auroka's hand, then turned to exit. "Coming, Inspector?"

Rana turned on her uncle. "All you asked for is gold?"

He shrugged.

"Well, not just gold," Wourinos chimed in. "He is also getting a full pardon for anything he has outstanding against him. And he really has the two of you, from what I understand, to thank for that."

"I no did nothin', Inspector. Should'a never been charged in the first place."

"Yes, well, I doubt that very much. But the law is the law, and you are no longer a wanted Frog." The inspector's face was a little sour.

Auroka brushed off the inspector, saying, "Oh, that's enough of that now. Never mind what was in the past. Surely we can let all that go now, can't we?" For all her playfulness, her tone was commanding.

Wourinos nodded. "Yes, I suppose I can. But if you'll excuse me, I should see the captain off." He gave a bow and exited with Captain Mourgan.

A smile sprang to life on Auroka's face as she looked over to her friends. "Who wants something to eat?"

Rana began to hop, but at the last instant remembered she was wearing a dress. Modesty won out over enthusiasm, and she settled for excitedly saying, "I do!"

They all laughed and Auroka showed them down a hallway. Rana's shoes clicked on the polished marble tiles of the floor. The Peste blinked happily as he flitted along beside them.

"You are, of course, free to stay as long as you like," Auroka told them. "But when you are ready to depart, I will arrange for you to have passage anywhere you would like."

"Thanks fer that. I think it be best iffn' we get Rana here back to Underbrook soon. I doubt her father know where she be."

"And will you be going back with her too?"

Brunois looked at his niece. "Aye, I will be."

Auroka nodded. "Well, perhaps when you are done there, you'll come back here? My father could use someone of your skills, I am quite certain of it."

"We'll have to be seein''bout that, I think. I'm no too certain I would want to be workin' fer yer father."

"What about working for me?"

Brunois croaked out a chuckle. "We'll have to be seein''bout that."

Rana bounded ahead of them, the Peste hot on her heels. She was finally starting to get the hang of walking in her new shoes. She threw open the doors of the dining room to see what awaited her there.

40

The train chugged along merrily. Brunois laid his head back against the seat and looked over at Rana. She was dressed in a pair of khaki trousers and white button-down shirt. "Much better for traveling," she had told him. He agreed. She looked different than she had a month ago when she had followed him to Dunham. Maybe he was just looking at her differently.

Probably both.

The late morning light was cheerful as it beamed through the windows of the train. The sky outside was cloudless, and the trees reached up at it, seeming to rejoice at being in the presence of the sun. Hat tilted forward over his face, Brunois drifted off to a light sleep.

He dreamed of his childhood. He played in the brooks and streams that surrounded the village with his brother, Arcator. They raced sticks through the small run of rapids by the bridge. They huddled around the fire at night, sipping hot cocoa and listening to Grandpop tell his wild stories of metal monsters and courageous soldiers. Rana appeared at one point, standing atop a hill and waving Brunois to come follow her into the woods. She called out to him, "Uncle Brunois! Uncle Brunois!"

He snapped back awake and looked up at Rana standing in the aisle. "Time to go, we're at the station."

The pair of Frogs disembarked to the platform, the Peste flying by Brunois's shoulder. Down below, a coach was already waiting to take them to Underbrook, courtesy of Lady Auroka Fiercheval. The ride only took a few hours and was done in relative silence. Both Brunois and Rana had a lot on their minds.

Arcator gonna be mad at me.

When they arrived at Underbrook, they elected to leave the coach at the bridge, wanting to walk through the sunset to the mill. Rana smiled as they moved through the familiar places of the village. The square, the well, the marketplace; they all filled her with a sense of peace, of security. There was no place like home.

As they passed the small church, Brunois stared up at the steeple. The building no longer looked cold and condemning but rather warm and inviting in the fading sunlight. He thought about Rana, lying lifeless in that streambed outside of Dunham, and the desperate prayer he had said.

Thank you. I guess.

The Peste flickered a few times.

Brunois looked over at the little brass firefly and nodded. "Yeah, I think ya be right."

The mill came into view. The sails spun lazily in the gentle breeze. Smoke rose from the chimney of the house in happy curls. A warm glow suffused the windows from the fire inside. The two travelers ascended the final steps of the front walkway and opened the door.

Arcator was sitting in a rocking chair by the fire, reading a book. He looked up. He jumped up. He ran over to Rana. "You're back! Oh, thank God you're back." He squeezed her until her little Froggy breath left her little Froggy body.

She said nothing in reply, just hugged him back. Tears streamed down both of their faces. They stood there for several minutes. Brunois stood off to the side, shifting nervously.

When Rana finally let go of her father, Arcator turned to Brunois. His eyes were big. His gaze was heavy. "Thank you."

Brunois balked. "Uh…ya be thankin' me? Fer what?"

"For letting her go with you, and for keeping her safe."

"Well, it just seemed like the right thing to be doin', is'all. I guess…" Brunois stammered and croaked as he tried to get the words out. He hadn't expected a thank-you. He also hadn't expected Arcator to step in and hug him. But he did.

Brunois hugged him back. He meant it this time. "Yer welcome, Arcator."

"And thank you too, Rana."

Rana raised a quizzical eyebrow. "Thank me? For what?"

"For leading my brother home. I thought he might never find his way back."

CHAPTER

41

"Ya sure ya don't wanna be comin' with us, Rana?"

"No, thanks Uncle Brunois, I don't feel up for fishing."

"Suit yerself then. I do." He grinned and disappeared from the door to her bedroom.

Rana heard his voice down the hall, saying, "Looks like it just be me and ya then, Arc." She smiled at the thought of her uncle and her father going fishing. The brothers were reconciled.

The sound of the front door shutting reached her ears as she lay in bed. *Boy, do I miss those goose-down pillows.* Nevertheless, it felt good to be home, goose-down pillows or not. She lay there a while and thought about what the future might have in store for her. They had received a letter from Captain Mourgan yesterday. The captain had been true to his word and arranged for her to study at the Royal Academy, as well as secured lodging for her in Chevaire.

Her mind rolled back over the recent past. She remembered the day her uncle had shown up, looking for the key in her great grandfather's things. *Why did he have it to begin with?* she wondered.

Rana hopped down from her bed and made her way to the root cellar, where she began searching for the trunk the key had come from. Arcator had put everything back after they had left, but with enough persistence, she was able to find it. She dragged it out and opened it. Inside were a soldier's uniform, a pipe, a compass, a pocket watch, and a number of other personal effects. Under a hat was the small wooden box that Brunois had found the key to the Peste in. She opened it to find a few sheets of paper that had been torn from a book. They were a journal entry.

June 17, 727 AE

God forgive me, but I just couldn't let them do it. The lieutenant had to be stopped. It was bad enough that Kaile had to lose his life in pursuit of this madness. I couldn't let them wake those things up and loose them on the world. I wouldn't even wish that on the Makivillaines.

The lieutenant came this morning and got some of the men, saying he was ready to try bringing the whole of the swarm to life. He knew better than to ask me. Especially after what had happened to Kaile. I was actually surprised he hadn't sent me back to the camp after that, but he was probably worried I would talk about what he was doing here and draw the attention of the colonel.

They all went down to the platform and began doing whatever preparations they needed to. I hung around at the edge of the tunnels, watching them from behind some rocks. Waiting for my chance. When they left for a moment to inspect the other clusters of metal eggs, I got it.

Remembering what Kaile had said, I ran out onto the platform and got down on my belly by the circle thing in the center. There were a whole bunch of handles around it that must be the valves he had been talking about. I turned them all back the other way and returned to my post.

They returned and took up positions at the different table-like things covered in switches. The lieutenant looked over the rest of the men and nodded, then prodded some of the devices he stood in front of. The great ball thing on the pedestal in the center of the platform started to shake and glow. The lieutenant looked very excited, right up to the point that a massive red glow shot up from under the platform and cooked all of them alive right where they stood. I felt the heat from it. It must have been awful for them. I watched them wiggle and flail about as their blood boiled inside of them. The ones that were just following orders I felt a little bad for, but I was happy to see the lieutenant burn like that. Served him right for what he was trying to do here.

Once I saw they were all dead, I ran up to the camp and told everyone that there had been an accident, that the lieutenant and the others had died while messing with that Svargan machinery, and we should go get help. I outranked all three of them, so they stepped in line, and we grabbed some supplies and made off. I took the egg that Kaile had been given, and a key he said that went with it. I figure it would at least give some explanation as to what happened here.

I know that when we report in, they're going to take my journal, so I'm tearing these pages out and taking this secret to my grave. They'll probably take the egg too, but I'm going to hide the key and tell them I don't know anything about any of it, I'm just a sergeant who was helping to guard the place. Hopefully they'll be too busy with the war to go investigate, and that place will just become lost again.

May God have mercy on me for all this.

EPILOGUE

Rana was late for class again. She glanced down at her pocket watch to see just how late. It told her.

Ugh. Ten minutes late. Professor Brioche is going to kill me.

She hurried down through the busy streets of Chevaire. Despite living here for some months now, she still found it hard to believe she was really here. The capital city of Marlebonne was massive to say the least. Old buildings of stone and brick were intermingled with newer ones of wood and steel. The citizens mirrored this eclectic mix, being even more diverse in their makeup. Rana had never seen so many different Species, let alone in one place. It had taken her some time to not gawk at some of them when she passed them on the street.

The walk from her apartment to the campus of the Royal Academy was only a few blocks. Captain Mourgan had been most generous with the arrangements he had made on her behalf, securing not only her tuition but very nice lodgings as well. Rent was usually quite high in this quarter of the city, and Rana would have felt bad were it not the Crown picking up the tab.

Loud voices echoed through the streets as she neared the common square of the academy. A large group was gathered, all facing a makeshift stage upon which a Frog was giving a speech. She wore a white dress with ribbons of violet and green around her head and arms, which danced with each gesture she made. The crowd was transfixed by what she was saying, although Rana was too far away to hear any of it.

"Rana! You're here!" The voice belonged to Harleigh, a Rabbit who Rana had become friends with since arriving in Chevaire. They were both taking a course of study on the Secession and Reformatory Wars.

"Yes, but I'm late for a class. I really can't stay…"

"Oh, but you must! Just for a moment, and here, take this." Harleigh shoved a pamphlet into Rana's hands. It was titled "The Return."

Before she could offer another protest, Rana was pulled bodily through the crowd by her friend. She tried to resist, but Harleigh overpowered her.

I didn't know dancers were so strong, Rana thought as she gave in and allowed herself to be dragged up front.

The speaker's voice boomed out over the crowd. "Has history taught us nothing? Are we not heading down the same path as the Svargans of old? Will we not yet turn from certain destruction?"

Enthusiastic nods rippled through the sea of heads. There were Foxes, Cats, Dogs, Lizards, Birds, Bears, and many other Species that Rana still did not recognize. Some of them called out their agreement, others simply yelled.

"We must forsake the technology that sows destruction! We must forsake the technology that reaps death! Now is the time! Do not be deceived by the empty promises of supposed progress! The world cannot survive another Great Cataclysm! Repent now, turn from the path of devastation while there is still time!" The Frog on stage punctuated each statement with a flourish of her hands, the colored ribbons swirling with the movements. Seeing that Harleigh was distracted, Rana slipped out from the crowd and hurried to Gilead Hall. She consulted her watch again.

Twenty minutes late!

She burst through the front doorway of the building and ran down the hall to the lecture room. With any luck, she would be able to sneak in the back and settle into a seat unseen. She cracked open the door and attempted to slide in noiselessly. Her luck ran out.

"So good of you to join us, Ms. Rana."

Caught.

"I was just about to explain the concept of chronotopic expansion and contraction. Perhaps you will find it to be useful knowledge in helping you to get to class on time."

Rana blushed and offered an awkward smile.

Professor Brioche smiled back at her. It was warm, and he paired it with a wink. "Now if you would please take a seat, we may continue."

She found the closest seat and slid into it, fumbling her rucksack open and taking out a ledger she used for keeping notes.

I hope he's right. I'm sick of never having enough time.

REFLECTION

The creative process has always been a cathartic experience for me. There have been many times in my life when artistic pursuits have helped me to wrap my head around things in my heart. As the words go onto the page, there is always that part of me in them, and as I go through the process of writing them, I learn things about myself and come away the better for it.

I went into writing this story with an idea of what I wanted it to be about, and while I worked, that idea grew, changed, and incorporated other ideas. Indeed, this book has turned out to be more than I could have hoped for, and I wanted to take a little time now to explain what some of this has meant to me.

Relationships

Relationship was the main theme I set out to deal with. Despite the high fantasy setting of a postapocalyptic, steampunk world populated by anthropomorphic Animals, my goal was to write a story that was character-driven. The idea was to demonstrate how Brunois learned the value of having relationships, and the work that went into cultivating them.

Brunois's name is a play on *brunoise* which is a culinary term referring to a very small dice (3 mm × 3mm × 3mm). His surname, Bonne'Chance, is French for "good luck" or "good fortune." This makes his name loosely translated, "a very small piece of good fortune." He is the character that most represents me, and his journey mirrors my own—that of a self-centered lout who comes to learn that relationships are critical to who we are as people. God has designed us to be in relationship with him and with one another.

Brunois starts out his journey concerned only with himself, but then Rana enters the picture and things begin to change. Something stirs in him, something he didn't even realize was there (or even particularly want to be there), but there it is. As the two of them go through their adventure, Brunois comes to care for her more and more and begins to see not only the value of having her around, since she helps in a practical way several times, but also the work that goes into having a good relationship. This work is symbolized by the Peste, as the little insect has to be wound daily. Sometimes he's helpful to Brunois, sometimes he's frustrating, but Brunois comes to dutifully winding his friend regardless. By the end of the story, he's moved beyond only doing that which benefits himself and started to walk in doing that which benefits others, for their sake alone.

The two scenes where the Frogs are settling in for the night, the first at the inn, the second in the jail cell, highlight Brunois's change of heart. The experiences he has had with Rana in between have transformed him, and with this new awareness, he is shedding his old nature. Rache is symbolic of this old nature, the two even having a similar manner of speech, and it is Rana who is instrumental in destroying this nature in him.

When Brunois finds Rana in the streambed after their final battle with the swarm, he prays for her. This is something very much outside of his usual beliefs, but in his desperation, he turns to this God he's heard about, and prays. He knows he doesn't have a relationship with God, or within the context of this world Eshua (a play on Yeshua, the Hebrew name for Jesus), but his prayer is answered anyway. God loves him despite his waywardness, just as he loves us. When his prayer is answered, it opens the door for further questions. Questions I plan on exploring more in my next book.

Brunois's whole character arc is very much a representation of my own. Rana would be symbolic of my wife, in that it was my relationship with her that taught me the value of having them. Not that I was aware of it at first, but when I found myself in a desperate time, where I thought I might lose her due to my selfish lifestyle, I came to realize how much I loved her, and my desperation to hold on to her opened the door for me to welcome Jesus into my own heart. Insofar as Rana then represents my wife (and they do share a certain spark in their personalities), the Peste would then represent my children. It was in experiencing my love for them that I learned how to show my wife how much I love her and learned that it is something that needs to be cultivated and tended to daily.

Gifts

We are all given gifts from God. Some of us are writers, some of us musicians, or athletes, or doctors, or leaders, or any number of other things. How we come to recognize, cultivate, and ultimately use our gifts is another theme I wanted to work with.

Rana has the gift of "fire." This starts out as something she wants no part of and only manifests it occasionally, and without much purpose or intent. We learn that because of an episode with her adoptive father, Arcator, she has viewed her ability as something bad and stuffed it down. Having words spoken to you by your father that caused you to view part of yourself as "wrong" is something I can certainly relate to, and sadly, I think many others as well. However, as she is given the opportunity to grow, and even in some ways be encouraged by Brunois, she comes to step into this gift of hers. By the end, she has not only come to accept it as a part of her that is good and special, but that she in turn has the responsibility of it. How she uses it matters, and when the time comes, she rises to the challenge of using it for the right reasons and begins to discover what it means to be a good steward of her talent.

Auroka, too, has been given gifts. She has birthright, education, and resources at her disposal. When we first meet her, we know only that she likes a life of adventure, much like our Frog friend Brunois. As events unfold, and more of her is revealed, we learn of how she has shunned the responsibilities of her life, but we also see that she is awakening to them as well. By the end of her time with Brunois and Rana, she begins to walk in her true identity. I often lament how long I spent running from who I am. Usually, it was because of a need, a void within me caused by some pain I couldn't articulate but was consumed by trying to alleviate. As I grew in my relationship with my wife, and with God, I have gradually come to not only accept, but rejoice in the things I have been called to, and have found true fulfillment in serving God, by serving others.

When I think about the gifts God has given me, I am humbled and a little ashamed at what I have used them for in the past. I have grappled with selfish behavior my whole life, and while I'm still on this journey of being perfected, I have to always be mindful that I am using what God has given me to do his work—using his gifts for his glory. This means not only being responsible with the abilities he has given me, but with the resources, and even more so with the people. The awareness of this principle is why I included this section in the book, that it might be part of my testimony to the reader.

A Light in the Dark

The title of the book refers to the journey of our lives. We each have one to walk, and it is very easy to get distracted by the things that surround us. Just as Brunois and Rana needed each other to find their way —him to seeing the value of relationship, and her to walking in her gift — we too need the support, encouragement, and sometimes correction of those around us. There are times when things can seem very dark, and we can be a light to one another. I am very thankful to have those people in my life who do this for me, and even more so, a God who loves me enough to do it as well.

Well, I sure hope you have enjoyed my little story! The whole experience of writing it has meant a lot to me, and I would like to thank everyone who has supported me in it. It is my hope that you, the reader, take something good away from it, and are enriched just as much in the reading as I have been in the writing. May God richly bless you.